A Mindful Death

By

Lars Bolin

For the "Angel" and "Snowflake" in my room

Lylian and Lynnea

Publisher: BoD – Books on Demand, Stockholm, Sweden
Printer: BoD – Books on Demand, Norderstedt, Germany
ISBN: 978-91-7699-443-6

The photograph reflects a moment that is happening out in the world, and also one that is happening in the minds of the photographer and the viewer. The fact that the moment is fleeing and will never get repeated ads to its appeal. A photograph acknowledges this transience.

The best ones match meaning to it."

David Butow

Prologue – Perugia, Italy in June of 2015

Leonardo

The photograph stared down at him from its spot on the wall.

After all these years, the pent-up feeling of having to live his life with a secret he couldn't share was released. With a long strenuous exhale he could finally take that deep breath of fresh air again.

He looked at it with tired eyes—eyes that had seen so much pain, so much hope vanish too many times. The feeling of tasting the end, almost making it and being so close as if he could smell the victory even before crossing the finish line.

Too many years had passed, living his life chained to a lie; a lie necessitating fits of action and forced inaction.

Many times he had felt shame, regret and suspicion of betrayal. It had troubled him to the point of wanting to

3

end it all; but when it came to a moment of clarity, there was too much at stake. Too many people depended on him sticking to the plan - the plan only he could see through, as if everyone else's success fell on his willingness and strength to carry on.

What if? The question he never could answer. The road he had traveled on was unpaved and one that never could, for security reasons, be paved. The only thing he could do was to travel along, keep going without looking back; without taking those exit ramps that had presented themselves to him over the years. It was painful every time he saw an exit sign, knowing very well he never could divert from the path. Now, at last, Leonardo's comingled tormented soul had finally reached the end of the road with tears and a smile.

He reached up, grabbed the photograph, and took a last look at it before crumpling it in his right hand; the same hand that had squeezed the trigger on a Lupara short barreled shotgun, so many years before.

He looked down at his fist, still firmly squeezed in a desperate attempt to free himself. Wanting to squeeze the life and lies the photograph emitted.

He was overwhelmingly tired. He placed his head on the soft pillow, closed his eyes and realized after having kept it all inside, behind a wall of silence, that, finally, he had told his side of the story and freed himself from the heavy burden he had carried around all these years.

Chapter One - April 3, 2015

Part I

Harry and Maria

Early spring -- one of those picture perfect days when life began again after a long harsh winter. Harry grabbed his Nikon D40. In terms of high tech, the camera was a relic. Yet it had served him well over many years of travel.

Harry had just turned 57 and was still in great shape thanks in part to his travels as a photojournalist. He reveled in the thought that he spent his time documenting all that he saw in pictures and words. Over a span of 35 years he tried many varied occupations. At first he served as a guard in a correctional facility on the West coast to more recently organizing and staging fundraisers for families in need on the East coast. In between, he had worked in the corporate world in many capacities.

Like a porcupine with his coat of sharp spines, each one of them reminding himself of the hostile environment where in he spent parts of his life, and how easily he realized, one could lose direction.

No, Harry was better off now. His many years as a "renaissance man" had provided him a myriad of talents and an understanding of life; things he now used, doing what he loved most.

Women had never understood Harry's rather complex view on life and in order to do what pleased him they often sacrificed a lot. He had never been able to sustain a long relationship, although there had been plenty of women wanting to put a stop to his wandering ways.

Harry wasn't the settling down kind of guy. He always seemed to find it more fulfilling and challenging to view life from different angles, those that most others would not consider. Sometimes it was an impression he wanted to capture in pictures or words. The challenge he fully enjoyed, of solving a problem or mystery that no one else paid heed to or knew how to approach. He was the man you asked when something needed to be fixed or when his friends needed someone with whom to vent. He constantly occupied his mind with new ideas and thoughts of how to look at life from different perspectives. He never really understood why people seemed to think that there was only one path to follow, or one way to proceed with their lives.

On this early April morning, he left his apartment at 22 West Street in Cold Spring, overlooking the Hudson River flowing from north to south through the eastern part of New York State and glanced over to "Storm King Mountain" for the weather forecast. The saying was that if the clouds were covering the peak of the majestic mountain in the morning hours, there would be a rain storm before the end of the day.

The writer, Nathaniel Parker Willis, who in the middle of the nineteenth century had taken up residence in the region, thought a proper name for the mountain was Storm King. Today, the sun covered the peak with no clouds in the clear blue sky. It certainly was going to be a great day for photography.

"Good morning Maria." Harry smiled and gave Maria a sideways glance as he entered her cafe.

"Good morning, my darling," she said with true affection. At age 56, Maria's face was still very beautiful and she possessed a well-proportioned body. She moved closer to Harry to catch the scent of his Mont Blanc after shave.

Maria was running her own café on Main Street, something she had done for over 30 years. It was the same café where she and Harry had met in as teenagers when the small shop was run by Maria's mother. They both worked there during their high school years and it was here that they lost their virginity on a summer evening after closing, before the start of their senior year.

Harry and Maria were a couple throughout the last year of school and made sure they closed the café on as many evenings as they possibly could convince Maria's mom to let them. Prom arrived and one last hot summer remained for the young couple before Harry was off to college on the west coast while Maria stayed and helped out her mom. The café was named Sweet Maria's Café—a sobriquet to her daughter.

"The usual?" Maria teased him, thinking back on those summers she and Harry spent working together and making love.

"Yes, same as last time, Maria." Harry responded with a tender smile on his face. "But make it a double, please."

"Sure, a large latte with double espresso shots coming up."

Maria took her time because she knew that was what Harry always wanted her to do. She always had an eye for him and the high school passion never dwindled; it just intensified over the years and made it more difficult to ignore. Time, thereafter, had too many boring and lonely evenings with or without her husband, Robert. It really didn't make a difference with him next to her in bed or not. Her thoughts had always wandered off in time.

She was unhappily married and now with grown children, she felt liberated. Her life as a café owner in town where everyone knew each other by first names had become boring over time. But every one of those mornings when Harry came in for his coffee after moving back to Cold Spring, she felt that urge to leave everything behind and start over. Maybe one day she would.

"Thanks Maria." Harry reached out to grab the large coffee she prepared with the usual heart shaped foam on the top. But this time he made sure he first touched her outstretched hand and time stopped for both of them. For a very short moment, they looked at each other with that same youthful, innocent expression they shared the first time they made love. And in that moment Maria thought to herself that the day had arrived to make the move and start over.

"You're welcome." Maria said with a voice that sounded both sad and excited at the same time. She let go of the mug, turned around and secretively put the hand Harry had touched up to her lips, her body reacted to Harry's scent as if they reached out for each other on the kitchen floor once again.

"Bye Maria, I'll see you tomorrow, same time. Have a great day," Harry said as he turned around and upon exiting did exactly the same move with his hand.

With his four dollar large hot latte, he walked out on Main Street, the same way he, in 1976 with a regular cup of 25 cent coffee had left her. It was a long time ago but he couldn't help thinking what life could have been had he chosen not to go to college on the west coast. Maria, with no other alternative than to stay home and help her mom, never got the opportunity to go to a college until later in life when she decided, at age 35, to get a degree in business. It was around that same time she took over the café from her ailing mother. Her marriage suffered from trying to run a café, taking night classes and keeping an eye on her two teenage daughter's activities.

The 80s drug scene had changed from the 70s when Maria and Harry used to smoke marijuana in the back seat of Harry's old Chevrolet Impala. It seemed more glamorous than that of her husband's and later her children's drug use. The problems facing her kids, while their dad seemed to stay away from home as much as he possibly could, gave her no time, nor desire, to be intimate with him when it so pleased him to show up. Many times, Maria thought he had affairs, and he probably did. Later they seemed to get along better, but the intimacy and sex had cooled off. She had many times thought about leaving him for Harry who never married. But Harry lived a life she never could at the time, with her responsibilities for the kids and a café she couldn't possibly sell. After all, it was named after her. How can you sell a café named Sweet Maria when you are that person?

Harry, who had lived all over the U.S., often found himself going back to Cold Spring in the summer, if only for a couple of weeks or occasionally longer. Since his early retirement at the end of 2014 from the corporate world, he relocated for good and the move stirred up those teenage feelings for Maria he thought were long gone and forgotten. Not by a long shot.

Part II

Joe

Harry walked up Main Street. He usually took the same route when his final destination was nearby Breakneck Ridge, a demanding trail but at the end a rewarding view of the lower Hudson River Valley. He had taken numerous hikes and pictures over the years and yes, many with Maria. The early mornings, before starting their summer jobs at the café, was always the best time to hike the mountain. Lying down in the grass on the evenings they weren't scheduled to close the café, they would stay a little longer on the mountain to smoke a joint and make love.

Today, on the spur of the moment, he stopped to say hello to his old friend and owner of Joe's Antique Store. Joe had moved to Cold Spring from the West coast after Harry and Joe met at the correction center back in the 80s. Joe, a drug addict who was stealing money to support his addiction, was in and out of jail like a busy shopper using the rotating door at one of the fancy department stores in the city.

When Harry found out after Joe's last release that Joe had a small business operation dealing in second hand furniture, vinyl records and CD's purchased from estates sales, Harry suggested a move across the US to Cold Spring. This way, Harry could keep an eye on Joe before his addictions completely destroyed his life.

At the time, Joe was sinking deeper into heroin and he could no longer control his intake. Harry spent a lot of hours outside his normal lifestyle trying to help Joe get back on his feet. It was as if no one else took the time to really understand Joe's problems, or for that matter, cared. When Harry did, it was a wake-up call for Joe to deal with his demons and start over. Joe never knew Harry's reasons for spending hours, day and night with him. But, ever since the day he started helping him, Joe felt forever in his debt and the two of them became friends. Albeit an odd friendship.

Back in college, Harry, like almost everyone on campus, was doing drugs. This was the late seventies and nothing was taboo. Drugs, sex and rock' n roll. It all blended in with the attempt to get a degree; something Harry succeeded in carrying out in part because he lost his best friend to an overdose of heroin in their junior year. That became his wake up call and he went cold on hard drugs.

He managed to successfully finish with a degree in Literature in 1980. Life was different back then, and now over 35 years later, Harry was looking back at the times of unrest as something that certainly had shaped who he had become and also had taught him some valuable lessons about helping others when help was needed.

Harry knocked on the door knowing very well that Joe was going to be there. He always was, even if the official operating hours were 11:00-5:00. Joe unlocked the door, the sign "Open for Business" still in clear view for

12

Harry to see. It was never turned over. Joe had this notion that if he did, he would be turning his back on the customers. Harry never turned his back on Joe. Instead he always seemed to be there to help, whenever and wherever Joe needed him. Cold Spring had become Joe's family and he knew that you do not walk away from your family and friends.

"Hey Harry! Great to see you. And I see you brought me a cup of coffee." He always teased Harry because the times Joe stopped by Harry's apartment to let him know about a new shipment of old postcards, he always brought Harry's favorite large latte with the one extra shot of espresso.

"Sorry my friend," Harry said. "Didn't plan to stop by today but saw you in the window so I wanted to see how you were doing."

Harry seemed to forget that he never brought any coffee, even if the visit was planned. Joe didn't mind of course. He was happy that Harry took the time to stop by. Not only because they were good friends but because Joe never wanted to bother Harry with any lingering problems, knowing that Harry had done more than anyone ever could for him over all these years. He did know that Harry always was there for him if needed but preferred when Harry stopped by on his own, knowing that he would always ask how things were going with both his business and personal struggle.

"So, what's going on today, Joe?" he wondered while casually sorting through the postcard boxes Joe had on the counter. It had become a routine at first, just to ease things up, not to stare Joe down as if he was on trial defending himself and his actions. Later, Harry had developed an interest in reading old postcards, some of which were post marked all the way back to the early 20s. There was so much to learn from them and the history of the families, their journeys, background, friends and everyday challenges.

Sometimes, if he was lucky, he found a whole box of postcards, all from the same family. Back in the days, with no telephones or at least a rarity to have one, communicating long distance wasn't as simple as just lifting up the handle and dial, or go online to shoot off an email. Nope, good old postcards were used back then to convey a message about what was happening, where you were and where you may be heading next.

"I'm glad you stopped by Harry." It seemed as though Joe wanted to tell his friend something that was a major issue on his mind. Since Harry had just come back from a longer than expected trip to Costa Rica, he hadn't seen him in over a month.

"Harry, do you remember that fellow back on the West coast I was "working" with?" Joe finally began talking after waiting for a lengthy period of time.

"Sure" said Harry, though he wasn't sure he wanted to remember. It was a guy closely affiliated with the mob.

"Well, he called me the other day." Joe looked up and starred at Harry with sober eyes; the same eyes that couldn't focus on one thing or person before Harry helped him turning his life around.

Harry looked at Joe with the usual, intense stare that he had used so many times over the years to fully understand what Joe meant to say, rather than what Harry heard him say.

"And…" Harry reluctantly added.

Joe was now looking away the same as he used to 30 years ago when he was embarrassed to confront Harry with his latest criminal offense or drug use.

"I don't know how he found me." Joe finally said after a long, tense, wait. "I mean it was no secret I left for the East coast but c'mon—he found me in Cold Spring!" "How is that even possible?" Joe was obviously upset.

"You know Joe, small towns are not necessarily the best hiding places although from what I know, you have nothing to hide." Harry replied thinking about his own love life with Maria that was never a secret in Cold Spring.

"I know." Joe sighed. I'm not happy about being "discovered" after all these years. Why is it that the past never seems to stop haunting me, regardless of how much

I want it to go away and want to start over. It's fucking unfair.

Joe's facial expression revealed the depth of his despair and left Harry with no doubt about how upset his friend had become.

"Ok Joe, so what did he want?" Harry felt obliged to ask even though the answer seemed rather obvious. "To start dealing drugs again?"

"No it didn't sound like it. That's what was so odd."

"Oh, c'mon Joe. What do you expect him to want from you other than being his East coast guy! Perfect cover, a former, now born again, drug addict hiding in a small town where no one knows your past - about the only thing this town doesn't know about you!"

Harry regretted his choice of words the second after he spoke them.

Joe looked at him with disappointment, rather than with anger...

"I think he wanted some information and he somehow thought of me." "Maybe because he knew where I lived and the information he needed was in this area of the East coast?"

Harry was taking it all in while trying his best to avoid reacting to what he thought he understood.

"So what are you going to do?" Harry thought about the day that started out so well with perfect spring weather for photography and hiking, Maria, still in love with him and life as simple as a decision about what to have for breakfast, was taking a turn for the worse.

"I fucking don't know, Harry." Joe seemed as lost as when Harry first met him over 30 years ago. It was then that Joe, leaning like a drunken sailor against the mast of his ship after yet another high, dialed the only number Joe was able to remember...Harry's.

"Well Joe...I'll tell you what I'd like you to do. You have been clean and stayed away from those guys for many years and I see no reason for you to get involved again in any way - you have nothing to hide, fear or lose by telling them to fuck off!"

It was rather obvious to Joe how furious Harry felt about the situation and right now Joe regretted having told Harry. It was unusual for Joe to feel that way. He always found it easy to confide in Harry about any serious and threatening situations in his life. For the first time he felt totally deserted and alone with his anguish.

"If it only was that easy Harry," Joe broke the silence.

Joe suddenly felt threatened by not as much his contact on the west coast as by Harry. What Joe never could understand was that whatever he had done in the past wasn't really Harry's problem or concern, but his alone.

17

Harry immediately regretted his outburst. He knew he had overreacted but wasn't prepared to have such a serious discussion with Joe on this beautiful morning when he had his mind set on a journey back to a joyous place, rather than dealing with Joe's problems once more.

"Well, Joe, let's think this over for a day or two. I'm not sure what good it would do to get involved with people you left behind so many years ago." Harry said trying to smooth things over.

Damn. It was as if he was getting down on Joe more than he already had. Again, he felt embarrassed to even think those thoughts. What was the matter with him? He was always there for anyone who wanted to talk, get help solving a problem or get back on their feet. He now seemed to turn Joe, a good friend, away when he needed him the most. Harry shrugged it off and decided that nothing was more important than being there for his friend.

"This is what we do, Joe." Give me the contact information for your guy on the west coast and I'll get in touch with him explaining that you are unable to reach out to him but that you asked me to call him back. And then we will see what happens. How about that?"

Unfortunately, Harry didn't think this through. He just wanted to get on with his morning. What did he just agree to? Contact a known mob guy on the west coast and ask him to leave Joe alone? But Harry just wanted to peacefully go back to those boxes of postcards, take that hike up Breakneck Ridge and lay down thinking about the times he made love with Maria. Just thinking about her he still felt aroused. Hell. He really messed it up back then.

"Thanks Harry." "You don't really need to do this." "I can take care of it myself." Joe knew and Harry knew this wasn't' true. Joe was as fragile as ever. Every day of staying away from drugs was a challenge, when his past seemed to catch up, like a dark shadow in a filthy alley, waiting to jump out and club him to make him come around and go back to the life he left. He was as helpless as that day, all those years ago, when he first met Harry.

Harry knew. And despite his wish to avoid the past and simply enjoy this beautiful April day, he would stop by to see Joe the next morning to get the contact information and make that call on behalf of his friend. But for now, Breakneck Ridge and more pleasant memories from the past with Maria were waiting.

Chapter Two

Harry didn't sleep much that night. Thoughts of the past he really didn't want to revisit had kept him awake. He mused about how to best help his friend Joe, without getting involved himself in what could be a messy and dangerous conversation with the west coast goon.

"Damn! Really, what can I actually do about Joe's predicament?" he said out loud to himself.

How much did Harry really know about Joe's past back and his involvement today? All he knew was 30 -year -old news! Maybe Frank (Harry remembered his name was Frank) was no longer involved in criminal activities. Maybe he, like Joe, had found a way out. Although, was there really a way out of the mob once you were in?

It was only 7:30 in the morning but Harry knew Maria was going to be at the café so he decided to use the back door and sneak in for an early latte and chat with her. It was yet another beautiful early spring day and he stopped for a few minutes by the river front and the gazebo to enjoy the view. The birds were singing and the morning light dressed up the mountain ridge on the west side of the Hudson River like a lace veil covering the beauty of the bride.

Maria turned around and immediately smiled when realizing it was Harry. Again, the memories from their senior summer year when they both arrived extra early in the mornings to spend the first half an hour together, reminded her about the boring life she now lived and had for some time. She thought about yesterday when Harry had looked deeply into her eyes for a split second leaving that special spell binding feeling that only Harry could evoke in her. And she decided, right then and there, that the time had arrived to make a move, a move long in awaiting. Her legs and thighs, that she had worked very hard to maintain in that same sexy shape she once had wrapped around Harry's inviting body, felt years younger.

"What a nice surprise," she finally was able to say after a while of staring at Harry, almost out of breath after her exciting day dreams from the past.

"I knew you would be here this early. I was on my way to Joe and after a bad night's sleep I really needed your latte with a double shot of espresso."

"Coming up my darling," Maria said in her usual but today more than ever loving, serious and meaningful voice. "Slow and steady like you always want it," she added and almost blushed saying it.

Harry moved up and stood just behind Maria, close enough for her to smell his after shave; the same one he had put on every morning since arriving back in Cold Spring to get his first latte of the day. Although not admitting to it, he was there to get his first morning glance at Maria.

Maria turned around and suddenly they were closer to each other than they had been since those summer days. Their eyes met, their faces close enough to smell and feel each other's breath, and their lips close enough to taste each other.

Harry was the one making the first move. He put his hands around Maria's neck, leaned forward and kissed her right below her left ear - the spot that brought her to her knees and sent signals throughout her body to want more of him. Maria gave up a sigh of delight and knew then that she could no longer resist. The only true love and passion she ever felt belonged to her High School sweetheart, Harry. She moved her right hand down Harry's spine while her left touched his still very muscular and broad chest, ever so gently touching his right nipple. A moaning gasp of delight came from Harry's mouth. Maria still knew the trick to get him excited and aroused although unnecessary on this very morning.

Things happened very fast. As if they were back in their teenage years, the clothes came off, their bodies intertwined on that same kitchen floor they had visited so many times, and Maria's sexy and lean legs and thighs were once more on top of Harry's eagerly awaiting erection.

"Slow and steady like you always want it." Maria heard herself saying as if to remind her that she didn't want this to end…ever.

Their love making was like a pressure cooker and the lid was about to release like a volcano erupting after years of being dormant. An orgasm was something very rare for Maria these days, and occurred only when thinking about Harry on those lonesome nights in bed. But now, having Harry once again, the dam was ready to burst.

Exhausted and satisfied they lay down next to each other on that kitchen floor they so many times had visited in the past - now a little bit more uncomfortable but they didn't mind because the satisfaction they felt was reward enough and any discomfort of being on a hard tile floor forgettable since nothing could in any way diminish the feeling of this special moment..

Maria was the first one to return to reality.

"We found ourselves back in time, didn't we," Maria said, again with her usual "my darling" added at the end of the sentence but now with a very special meaning to it.

"I know, Maria." Harry leaned over to kiss Maria but she turned away as if she wanted to avoid him. Instead she grabbed his hands, held them tight and got down on him, wanting him one more time in case this would be the last time they got the chance to make love. The same intense feeling and fear she had back then when he left for college, never to return to her the same way. She wanted to feel complete, if only for one last time. She felt his manhood grow during her skillful and playful act. She had not forgotten the things that used to drive them both crazy with lust.

"Slow and steady," Maria moaned.

"Like you always want it," Harry added before he, despite his age, but thanks to his physique, picked up Maria and pushed her against the kitchen wall with her beautiful, slender and sexy legs wrapped around him.

"Oh, Maria!" he was able to say before the excitement of once more being inside her took over and made them both come again.

Thirty minutes later, Harry was sipping his by now cold, but still very tasty, latte while Maria was preparing to open the café for her morning customers.

"What about dinner one evening, Maria?"

"Would love to, Harry."

That settled it. They were not going back to anything less than what they both knew would be theirs to keep now. The dull and in many ways non-existing love life of Maria's past was over and for Harry, he was finally back where he knew he belonged.

"Ok, great! Tomorrow night I'll take you down to The Half Moon in Dobbs Ferry!"

Before Maria could stop him, he kissed her at the exact moment the first morning customer entered. Luckily Mrs. Rose didn't even notice them and that was a good thing because if there was anyone in the village who made sure she knew everything and made certain everyone else got informed about the latest gossip, Mrs. Rose certainly was the one.

The early April air outside Sweet Maria's Café felt like a cold shower when Harry stepped out. He took a deep breath, turned around to glance at Maria through the glass entrance door as she served Mrs. Rose her usual coffee, no milk but three spoons of sugar. What a waste of Maria's great coffee, he thought to himself. He took a sip of his now cold latte, the heart still visible on the foam.

Happier than he had felt for a long time he strolled up Main Street to Joe's. His problems were no longer like the steep hill Harry had envisioned yesterday but rather like mounting a stallion - exciting, challenging, with the ultimate goal of taming the wild "beast" on the west coast who somehow thought it was ok to engage Joe to start dealing after all those years of staying away.

"Good morning Joe!" Harry cheerfully, with the satisfaction of someone who just had gotten laid, almost screamed out the words.

"Oh, Hi Harry." Joe turned around quickly from behind the counter, surprised and with a sweeping move put something back in the cash register before closing it.

Harry didn't think about it then, but later he recalled the episode and could have sworn that what he saw was Joe putting a revolver in the drawer.

"You startled me Harry." Joe seemed a little off this morning as if he hadn't slept that well either.

"Not much of a sleep last night, huh?" Harry said looking at him with the same tired, but a lot more excited eyes. After all his morning had started off with a visit to a past much more pleasant than the one Joe and he were about to discuss now.

"I thought about what you said yesterday." Joe didn't look up, avoiding eye contact with Harry. "And I have decided I better call up Frank myself." "It really isn't for you to do."

Harry was relieved but at the same time curious and he wasn't going to let this pass by without knowing what Frank wanted.

"If that is what you would like to do, Joe." Harry couldn't believe he felt disappointed not being asked to make the call. "But let me be present when you call, would you?" he asked with a degree of desperation in his voice. Harry felt like something very interesting was about to happen. He didn't know why but his rather well developed sixth sense told him so. Now, as if yesterday's hesitation and lack of sleep over Joe's predicament never happened, he felt excited about the whole thing. Maybe it was Maria that had awakened the passion for adventure - the desire to find a new reason to leave the cozy small town life of Cold Spring for a while.

With a glance over at the cash register, hoping Joe kept the register open or just to confirm that he really had put something back, Harry left the store puzzled by Joe's sudden decision to call Frank himself. The mysterious behavior behind the counter when he had walked in on him earlier, just added to his curiosity. It is funny, Harry thought to himself, how the past, when creeping up on you has a tendency to change everything in a heartbeat. It's like the past isn't the past but rather a dark corner of the brain; a very present and integral part of your soul and a shadow that follows wherever you go and whatever you have done in life.

Then, when you least expect, it hits you in your face, like a jack in the box.

Chapter Three

Winter was back. It had snowed all night and in the early morning hours when Joe got up, he looked out his bedroom window on a village dressed in a Winter Wonderland costume. It felt more like Christmas than spring.

"Fuck!" The only word Joe could think about saying as he shook his head in disgust. The frustration of once again being fooled by spring and hopes crushed that a new beginning was about to unfold. Winter had returned though and still held its grip over the small town and the people who desperately wanted to escape hibernation. The snow had, at least temporarily, held back the birds that only yesterday were serenading spring.

"Things looked so much brighter yesterday." Joe continued to talk out loud, something he had started doing during his long and lonely prison days when he didn't interact with another human being for hours, sometime days. What wasn't clear to Joe was if he was speaking about the weather or his own misfortune of having encountered Frank from his past. Yesterday, after Harry had walked in on him putting the revolver away in the cash drawer; the one Frank had asked him to get rid of a long time ago, but never did, he had looked back at the life he once lived but had left behind. Or, at least he thought it was part of the past. Now he wasn't so sure anymore because he would never be free as long as it kept asking for his attention, demanding favors that he didn't owe anyone any longer.

"Shit!" I'll just call the bastard today and ask him to fuck off! That's what I'll do." Joe, still talking to himself like he wanted to tape record his conversation, rewind and listen back to his own stupidity!

Joe again felt lonely, scared, confused and angry; all at the same time. He kept telling himself over and over that Frank just wanted to catch up, nothing else.

"I'm sure it's a simple request or question of some kind," Joe muttered out loud. "I've got nothing to hide so why am I freaking out?"

Humans, unlike animals, hide things when we feel uncomfortable. Animals just "attack" anything that gets in their way and deal with the consequences later. No waiting, no looking back, no regrets. Joe had had plenty of time putting his criminal past behind him, locking it up in one of those dark corners of the brain and throwing away the key. His involvement with the mob on the west coast was 30-year-old history, but today he realized someone had found the key to unlock all the bad memories. Actions he didn't deem acceptable for a man of his stature today, but rather the animal he had once been and who back then had decided that the best defense was to strike first and fast.

Rather than the usual sixty seconds it took to walk down the steps from his upstairs living quarters to the shop downstairs it took a long five minutes. He kept stopping and returning back upstairs only to realize he couldn't turn away from his past. He needed to strike with force so that it wouldn't come back ever again. The instincts, the justification and pleasure of using force when and if necessary to get what he wanted or needed, had returned. It reminded him of the reason for taking the revolver out of his safe yesterday.

Once down in his store, he stared for the longest time at the telephone as if he expected it to automatically punch the numbers. After what felt like an eternity, he picked up the phone, took a quick look at the postcard he used yesterday to scribble down Frank's number, dialed and took a deep breath. What's next he thought? He held on to the handle with a firm grip as if he was holding on to a weapon. One ring, two rings, three rings…no answer…four rings…still no answer…Joe took a deep breath of relief. Maybe he got the wrong number. Maybe it was just a prank call from Frank who wanted to scare Joe into believing he was "on the hook" with the mob again. Five rings…Joe was about to hang up when a voice suddenly broke the silence.

"Hey, it's Frank. Who the hell are you?"

Joe started to sweat even though it was freezing cold in his office.

"Hey Frank, its Joe. You called me--remember?" Joe was hoping he wouldn't remember and that it all was one big misunderstanding.

"Do you know what fucking time it is?" Frank was screaming. "It's fucking four in the morning!"

Joe started to shake. Not only was he scared to death to talk to Frank but now he had inadvertently awakened him at four in the morning. He had forgotten the damn time difference! It was seven in the morning in Cold Spring and Joe assumed everyone was up at this hour, not thinking that at four in the morning west coast or east coast time most people were asleep.

"Oh, I'm so sorry Frank. I didn't realize the time difference." Joe felt like he was about to pee on himself.

"Well, you got my attention. After all who wakes up Frank at four in the morning if it isn't for some really good news?"

Joe really needed to go to the bathroom to throw up.

"Hey Frank, it was great hearing back from you yesterday after all these years," he finally got the balls to say. Joe lied, but having spent 15 years with an addiction and a criminal record that spoke volumes, he had out of necessity picked up this unfortunate skill.

"I'm glad you feel that way, Joe," Frank replied with a grin on his face that Joe, even though he obviously couldn't see it, felt all the way from the west coast to Cold Spring.

Both Joe and Frank were wide awake now. Joe nervously waiting for the next move by Frank who now realized he had Joe's full attention and could do what he did best - go after the prey like a wolf.

Frank had met Joe back in the mid-80s at a cocktail party in Las Vegas hosted by the LA mob boss John Broglio. Joe, the gambler, as well as the drug addict he was, had been approached by Frank on numerous occasions back then because of his losing streak at the black jack tables and the rather substantial debt he had run up over the years. Frank had close ties to Broglio's gambling business and had been told to keep an eye on Joe.

Harry had always wondered what Joe had done to get Frank and the Broglio mob family off his back. Joe's numerous imprisonments were mostly minor offenses - burglary, drug use and gambling - but Harry had always suspected there was more to it.

Despite all the support he had provided Joe over the years he never got close to finding out why suddenly Joe was able to walk away, move to the East Coast and until now never been bothered by his past associates.

Obviously, he didn't really know Joe that well. The friendship was an odd one and more so, a result of Harry's determination to help Joe get back on his feet – It gave him a pleasant feeling of accomplishment knowing he had succeeded in turning at least one ex-con around out of the many he had come to know.

"So Joe," Frank said with a voice that sounded like he was going to lecture his friend, "It sure was a long time ago but family sticks together, right?"

Joe could feel his heart pounding as if it wanted to escape his body and seek shelter somewhere safer.

"What the fuck!" Joe said to himself while desperately trying to collect his thoughts and sound calm, using his street smart past and instincts to fight off a threat.

"Yeah, guess that's so." "That is if the family does stick together day in and day out and don't run away from its responsibilities." Joe couldn't believe he actually spoke to Frank with such ballsy conviction. The adrenalin rush of fighting back kept him going and he was just about to add another blow to Frank's reference to a family Joe hadn't heard from for over 30 years, when Frank interrupted him.

"Don't you fucking talk to me like that, "little" Joe!" he screamed into the telephone and the sheer force of his spitting mad voice hit Joe like a punch in the gut.

Frank had numerous times called him little Joe, "a name befitting a 5' foot 2" balding piece of shit!" as he liked to refer to him, even in front of the family members the times Joe had been summoned to appear to explain his black jack winning streaks and later, once he ran out of luck, the gambling debts.

"You listen to me now," continued Frank.

Joe said nothing. After years of silence, forgetting how low one can sink, he wished the phone had never rung the other day or he never returned the call this morning. He was screwed and had no way of escaping the iron fist of the west coast mob, even after all these years. He gave in. The instinct of fighting back was gone, like spring that abruptly had been interrupted by the return of winter earlier in the morning.

"I'm sorry Frank," he finally got the courage to say. "I know how good the family was for me back then and I haven't forgotten."

Joe was tamed again. His barking, like a stray dog without a family or home, had been silenced by the roar of the lion from the west coast.

"What is it you want me to do Frank?" "You know I'll do anything for you."

Joe was ready to throw up again - this time it wasn't the fear but the shitty feeling of having been deflated and defeated. He really felt like that little piece of shit Frank had told him he was all those times back then.

"Glad you realize that once a brother, always a brother."

Joe was about to say something but knew it was useless to fight back. Brothers in crime maybe, but no brotherly love here he quietly muttered, as if he was still talking to himself, not realizing Frank was still on the other end listening in. Oh shit, did he hear me? He gasped and waited.

"Joe, what are you fucking muttering about? I can't hear you! Speak up you little bastard!"

Neither said a word. The silence felt like an eternity. It was like time had stopped and they found themselves back to those days in Vegas when the night turned into daybreak but no one cared as long as the cards and the money was up on the table ready to be dealt and won.

Joe was the first one to break the silence. The nocturnal lifestyle he lived during his involvement with the mob had been replaced with a much nicer one where day and night mattered. Was it a dream though? Had he really gotten away from Frank and his boys? Was he having a bad dream? The ones you wake up from drenched in sweat because it felt so real, then relieved to know it was only a bad dream. If his last 30 years living a peaceful small town life was a dream, he didn't want to wake up from it.

"I just said I'm happy to reconnect with my family again." Joe lied with a conviction in his voice that even fooled him. "What is it you want me to do Frank?"

Joe opened up the cash register to hold the revolver as if by doing so he felt more important and empowered than Frank. Joe's mind was racing. Grabbing on to the gun helped him feel stronger and in his mind, he pointed it at Frank. He was in control and the trigger could go off any time he felt threatened or simply when he felt like it. That raw animal survival instinct, attacking the enemy while you still had the upper hand was a very real and powerful feeling. In the past he had felt it many times when doing the dirty work for "la famiglia."

"Joe, my brother," Frank started saying as if he meant it. "I have a job for you."

Joe held onto the gun, finger on the trigger, ready to kill. He felt the adrenalin pumping the blood faster through his veins, making him dizzy.

"And what would that be?" he finally asked. Joe feared the worst.

"I have a photograph of the past in my possession and I need you to help me find the people in the picture!"

Chapter Four

Harry overslept. Maybe it was the excitement from yesterday's steamy reconnection with Maria. Maybe, never mind the sex, he simply felt exhausted for having taken a leap of faith; a move he should have had the guts to do a long time ago but was too afraid of. Did he feel worthy of Maria? Of course he did! He knew very well how attracted Maria was to him but until now he had never admitted to himself how attracted he was to her.

Harry was a very private person. He lived a Hollywood lifestyle, perfect from the outside but rather lonely once you started to scrape the surface. He feared he would lose his independence if he let someone in too close; too personal.

He rolled out of bed, took a quick look outside at the returning winter weather and thought to himself that his winter collection of photos were about to get a few extra, not planned, additions. He glanced over at the mirror where his Nikon D40 was hanging as if to tell the camera to be ready for another hike later.

He stopped by the mirror, took a long good look at himself, making sure he really was looking at Harry; the man who stayed away from anything that could keep him tied to one place, one woman. His appearance was important to him although the mirror wasn't as friendly as it once was. No matter. He felt good about what he saw.

Harry always slept naked even in the cold winter nights of the Northeast. Most of the time though he found travel writing gigs somewhere in the southern hemisphere when northern temperatures crept below 32 degrees. But this morning he stood there, his hair still thick and dirt blond, not gray, looking at himself in the mirror.

"I feel great, I look great and yesterday I had sex with Maria on the café kitchen floor like we used to in the old days," he happily mumbled to himself with a big smile on his face. It was like he had to convince himself that what he was about to do was the right thing. Even for a man like him who thought he never would settle down.

He laughed, flexed his muscles and decided to wait for his shower until after his hike. Tonight was his big date, taking Maria down to The Half Moon restaurant in Dobbs Ferry, and he wanted to make sure he looked his best. He reached out for his Tommy Hilfiger briefs and put on a t-shirt and pants. It seemed fitting to wear Dockers. He traveled, lived a very active life and the pants made him look younger.

*

Joe's eyes were glued to the computer screen. Frank had told him he was going to email the photograph. Joe, eager to get this behind him and go on with his life, knew he was on the hook to do this favor. He hated it but had no choice, considering the favors given to him thirty years ago. His once lucrative drug dealing on the west coast, using the cover of his second hand furniture business and protection by the mob, had given him a chance to pay back his gambling debt to the Broglio family.

When Don Dominic Broglio died in 1984, Joe was given a "free-pass" from Frank to move on and along with the help from Harry, he was able to break free and start a new life on the east coast. Of course, drugs were only one of many illegal and brutal favors he did when tied to his gambling and drug use debts. Had no choice but to do whatever he was told.

He wanted to make sure Harry didn't get more information about his past than he already knew. But he still wanted to use him and his eagerness to help. He knew Harry couldn't say no to an adventure that involved traveling. Joe was pretty sure whatever Frank was going to send him wouldn't be solved in the small town of Cold Spring. Time after time Joe had wished he never had done what he did but it was too late to do anything about it. It just pissed him off that after thirty long years without any illegal activity other than avoiding Uncle Sam's long outstretched tax hand, he was once more involved with the mob. He shrugged off his thoughts with a smile thinking he wasn't the only one in Cold Spring who was running away from the IRS.

You've got mail started to flash on the screen in front of him. As if he was going to defuse a bomb, he carefully and only after taking a deep breath opened up the email from Frank. The subject line was empty with an attachment and a short text message - "Find them!" He opened up the attachment and what he saw surprised him.

It looked like a really old picture and not the kind he had expected to see. It seemed like a family photo of a mother and a father with their three children. Joe didn't know what to make of it first. There was a second attachment and Joe opened it. It was the back of the photograph with a date - July 17, 1945 and the word "ARRIVATI" written next to it.

Joe knew what to do. He printed the front and back of the picture for Harry.

Harry had just put his slacks on when the phone rang.

"This is Harry," he said with a broken morning voice. No coffee yet. I need that coffee he thought to himself.

"Harry! It's Joe. I hope I didn't wake you up?" he said without meaning it.

"Not a problem Joe. I'm just on my way to Maria for my morning latte. Can I stop by right after? I overslept and I desperately need that caffeine kick, you know."

"Sure, that works Harry. I've got something I'd like to show you and it is fucking old just like you!" he couldn't help himself saying. It was a relief to speak to Harry after the less pleasant conversation he had earlier in the morning. Harry was always a good sport and replied:

"Just because you're two years younger than me doesn't mean you look younger!" Very well aware of his physical attributes and next to the short, thin haired and overweight Joe, Harry felt like a movie star.

40

"Alright, rub it in!" Joe said laughing. It felt great to laugh. The feeling of wanting to throw up was gone. Knowing Harry would take an interest in the picture had helped him get off that dark path with no lights and no end in sight. Frank, after all these years of staying away, had crashed into his life again, and taken away the pride and self-esteem he had worked so hard over the last 30 years to redeem.

"I'll be over soon, Joe." Harry interrupted Joe's flashback and hung up on him even before Joe got a chance to respond.

Caffeine next.

Thinking that he wouldn't mind something more than just coffee this morning he realized it was too late for any morning adventures. He had overslept and Maria's café was already open. Tonight though he was taking Maria to dinner in Dobbs Ferry and who knows what the dessert is going to be he thought when locking the door behind him. He started up the street to catch his first cup of coffee of the day in the wintry and cold weather that had swept in over the Hudson River Valley for, hopefully, the last time this season.

"Shit, I forgot my jacket," he said out loud, having gotten used to not wearing one when the birds were serenading spring instead of today's snowflakes falling on his t-shirt covered chest. He turned around, went back inside to get his winter jacket that was hanging in the hallway. Harry wasn't much of a believer in fate but usually kept his winter clothes in plain sight until May. This way he was safe from any unpleasant surprises like this morning's sudden change of weather. He quickly grabbed his Nautica duffel jacket, a pair of gloves, scarf and Nikon D40, deciding at the spur of the moment to take a few more winter pictures while the snow was fresh and white. He had been traveling most of the winter and now after a month long stay in Costa Rica he actually didn't mind the snow covered streets and mountains across the Hudson.

Maria, who looked more radiant than ever this morning, prepared Harry's latte while at the same time getting a couple of customers who waited in front of him their regular coffees. It was a busier than usual morning due to the return of colder temperatures. The snow always seemed to be a good reason to start the day with a special coffee drink, rather than the home brewed boring black mixture.

They didn't say a word to each other this morning as if yesterday's physical pleasures had somehow cemented an understanding that no more flirting was necessary. What a shame if that was the case. Flirting is what keeps a relationship exciting and fresh. This was obvious yesterday when their eyes met and that inexplicable understanding and common universal language of passion replaced their words. Something else was different as well. Harry didn't notice it until he had paid and stood outside the café taking his first sip of the hot latte with a single shot of espresso. Instead of the usual one heart shaped in the foam, Maria had taken the time to make two. Harry smiled, looked around and waved back to Maria through the window. Maria returned his wave with a blow kiss and a smile. They couldn't wait for tonight's dinner date. It was going to be a great evening - they had waited a long time for this to happen and they both wanted it more than they could ever have imagined.

Chapter Five

Harry took a few snapshots of the snow covered windows along the way up to Joe's. The window displays of some of the boutiques or the simple, dusty and dirty windows of some of the antique stores told stories of hardship, beauty and success. Harry had always been fascinated with the stories they were telling. Now, like the accented lines in a drawing, the snow added the light and shade that helped create the true expression of the object. And by capturing the moment using his camera, the artist's pencil, he immortalized not only the town he grew up in but ensured that future generations would capture pieces of its history and beauty.

Harry went up to Joe's door, peeked inside through the window and saw Joe waving at him to come in.

"What's up Joe?" Harry wondered after taking a quick glance at him, noticing the printout of a picture in his hand, and the worried look on his face.

"Summer beige pants with a winter coat and sneakers in this kind of weather!?" "I'm disappointed" Joe continued in disgust but smiling with his whole face.

"Not one of my proudest moments" Harry said while looking down at his odd choice of clothes for a day when winter had returned with a vengeance.

"Take that snarky smile off your ugly face!" said Harry, happy to see Joe smile. This was a rare sight since most of the time Joe looked like he had all the troubles of the world on his shoulders.

"I spoke to Frank." Joe broke the pleasantry in a slow motion like voice because he felt like it took a lot of guts to say the words.

So he did call and didn't ask me to be there like I'd asked, Harry thought to himself, not surprised but still a little disappointed by Joe's decision.

"What did Frank say?"

Joe wasn't eager to reply. He had really not thought through what he was going to say to Harry, or what not to say. Instead of replying he stretched out his right hand holding the front and back paper copies of the photograph he just had received and printed out.

"Frank sent me these," he finally said. He waited for Harry to examine the photograph. A couple of times Harry looked up at Joe as if to say something but quickly turned his attention back to the print-outs he was holding in front of him.

"You weren't kidding - this photo looks like it was taken a long time ago."

"Yeah, take a look at the date on the back of the picture. July 17, 1945."

Harry was intrigued. He was also surprised to know that Frank had gotten in touch with Joe, not about dealing drugs again it seemed, but to show him a picture of a family dated back seventy years.

"Joe, what is it that Frank wants you to do with this picture?"

"Just locate them, he said."

"How are you going to locate a family from 1945 without any more information than a picture?" Harry was sure he had not heard the whole story and wondered what else Frank had asked Joe to do.

"That's why I called you right away. If anyone loves to solve a mystery it's you." Joe answered with such conviction that he surprised not only himself but Harry as well.

"Well," Harry, who had a weakness for flattery almost blushed. "I certainly do but this is not much to start with" he continued already preoccupying his brain with the mysterious family, why the photo had ended up with Frank, the writing on the back of the photo, and why Frank, so interested in finding out who they were, where they are or were last seen, found it necessary to call up an old associate, after all those years in hiding to help him.

"So you'll help?" Joe cracked his knuckles while waiting for Harry to answer. It was a habit he picked up while gambling; a diversion from the reality he didn't want to face.

"Of course I will Joe." What else could he say? He always wanted to help, and God knows he had over the years. But what it always came down to was his never ending thirst for adventure and mysteries. How could he turn away a chance to find the identity of a family with only a picture of them, two words, four names and one date going back seventy years?

"But this isn't really much to start with. Did Frank tell you anything else, like why now, why you?"

Joe hadn't really thought about asking. He knew that when Frank called, he still owed him, even after thirty years. What was painfully clear to him was that Frank didn't just want him to find the "bastards" but, if still alive, kill them. Harry would never understand what it is like to live your life in fear of being asked to do certain things you must do, to protect your "family". As much as he hated being trapped in this invisible bond, he was, and could do nothing about it. Even when "released" from his obligations, it wasn't a guarantee for life and when the boss told you what to do, you did it. No questions asked.

"No he did not. I guess the family in the picture arrived to New York back then and I being here on the east coast…," Joe answered without finishing the sentence, looking straight at Harry as if to convince him with not only words but body-language that there was no more to it than that. Joe knew he had Harry on the hook. Harry couldn't turn down an adventure and mystery like this one so he felt confident that the family would be located. Not by me, he thought to himself…but by Harry. And once he finds them, I'll be there to finish up. He smiled. Let Harry do the legwork, put all the clues together and Frank would never know that anyone but I was behind it all. A smile was plastered all over his face. "Smart thinking Joe, smart thinking…" he thought to himself.

Chapter Six

After Harry left Joe that morning he went about doing his winter photo session - the last one for the season. Using the back drop of the rather empty streets of Cold Spring he captured the purity and innocence of the white snow, covering the windows of the many antique stores and houses in the village he grew up in. His thoughts were drifting like the snow in the wind between his next two challenges in life; the photograph and Maria.

Maria was different. Not only because she was his first love, and very likely his only love, but more so the way they reconnected so passionately and suddenly. He was excited but also scared. This was new territory and he felt for the first time, he couldn't allow this woman to slip through his fingers – the way she once did.

The thought about the photograph ended his daydreaming, and on the spur of the moment he decided to talk to her about the picture. The thought surprised him but it also made him feel more at ease that he had something to share with her, other than just the usual chit-chat over dinner. Obviously he would have to leave out a lot of his conversation with Joe. He would just tell her how he found the picture at Joe's store while sorting through old postcards.

*

The sun had come out again and the snow was quick to melt in the rather strong early April sun. It looked like the evening was going to end in more spring like weather and lively conversation rather than this morning's wintry conditions and the serious discussion with Joe. After swinging by the Cold Spring Liquor Store on Chestnut Street for a bottle of wine he settled down in his favorite chair at home with a glass of Chardonnay before taking a refreshing shower. He was nervously awaiting the strike of eight when he had promised to pick up Maria.

Maria's husband was once more nowhere to be found and at this point Maria could care less. She was as excited as Harry to feed their passion with a seafood dinner at the beautifully located Half Moon in Dobbs Ferry. Maria had closed the café an hour earlier to the dismay of the ever present Mrs. Rose who had been knocking on the door window until finally Maria came out from the kitchen to tell her that she had decided to close early. After the morning winter rush, and when the sun came back in the late afternoon, no one was in a rush to pick up coffee drinks - except Mrs. Rose of course who lived on coffee and gossip.

There was only one person in Maria's thoughts at present and it caused her to smile in anticipation.

"You look fantastic." Harry was punctual for a change. His Volvo, a relic from his Swedish heritage, had received its first spring cleaning and looked five years younger than the 2005 model it was. Maria, who was the one to whom the compliment referred to, walked up to the passenger seat and got in. Harry closed the door, he, like the gentleman he was, had held it open for her.

"Thank you," she said as she crossed her legs, strapped the safety belt over her bare shoulders and the sexy low cut cleavage of the red evening dress she had found hanging in her closet. She felt like she was back in that old Plymouth Barracuda Harry had seduced her numerous times on those hot and steamy summer evenings back then. She felt young, seductive and yes very eager to get on with dinner, already having decided on dessert. No menu necessary. Finally she had found what she had been looking for almost her whole life. At this point in her life she didn't care as much about how she had wasted so many years on a man who never knew how to treat a woman, than how much she was looking forward to the years ahead with a man who knew.

She suddenly recalled the Iron Maiden lyrics "In your eyes I see the hunger, and the desperate cry that tears the night" from their song, "Wasted Love". It was a hit about the same time she had given up on her husband. It was right after she had finally received her long overdue degree in business and had taken over the café from her ailing mother.

She wasn't really an Iron Maiden fan, far from it. She, like Harry, loved almost all kinds of music, from opera to rock n' roll, but hard rock and rap were both taboo in her CD collection. So it was no surprise to her when Harry put a romantic classical music in the CD player of his aging Volvo and drove off. She smiled and placed a kiss on Harry's right cheek.

"You better not," Harry reluctantly replied to her nonverbal display of affection. "Let's make sure we get down to Dobbs Ferry and dinner in one piece." He smiled and felt so much better now than he had in many years.

Throughout the thirty-minute ride down south along the river banks of the Hudson Valley not many words were spoken. It was as if they both, in their minds, were going over the past almost forty years and how they could have been in denial as to not make any effort to rekindle their romance until now.

While "Passione" sung by Mario Frangoulis streamed out from the speakers, Maria glanced over to Harry, who quickly turned towards her with a big smile on his face, without losing focus on the road in front of him. Maria thought about the years she had spent with Harry before he went to college and the last twelve months that had passed after he moved back to Cold Spring. Not as much about what they had done but rather how he hadn't changed too much over the years. His slim, tall body; the way he spoke, rather slow and methodically as if he was thinking ahead what to say next before speaking; his movement using his length to his advantage, almost running rather than walking; and his warm and loving personality that was screaming I want to help.

Her eyes moved from his wonderful sexy lips that so many times had done the job on her neck, right below her left ear, to his green eyes fixated on the road in front of him. That smile of his that had done the trick many times with her, and, she assumed, a few other women over the years, was a warm and sincere smile, a smile you couldn't resist reciprocating with a smile back. She had always been surprised though how animated Harry became when excited and challenged. The competitive side of him was in hiding for most of the time but when challenged he always came out roaring like a lion who had been caged up for far too long. Funny, she thought to herself, how much in control he is until the very passionate and romantic part of him completely takes over.

At first he comes out like a rather reserved loner who seemingly cares less about the people than the action around them. There always seems to be something interesting that catches his attention rather than the people themselves, she thought while scanning over his well-built muscular yet slim body. But once you got to know him, he was not only a very charming but also loyal and devoted to the people who deserve his love.

She considered herself very lucky to have gotten to know the real Harry, and even more so now that the misery of losing him had been replaced with the explosive joy of reuniting with the man of her dreams. Yes, the Harry I know, she thought, is the same Harry I fell in love with once before.

Harry stared at the road in front of him. He couldn't avoid noticing how Maria was checking him out and he, while listening to "Passione", felt flattered, excited and nervous all at the same time. Am I, Harry Anderson, really ready for this. My God, it was just yesterday we made love on the kitchen floor but it felt like it was the first time.

I couldn't believe how quickly we seem to have gotten involved once again. But to have that same exciting feeling return at my age and with a woman I once was madly in love with. What are the odds?

He smiled one of his warm, friendly and inviting smiles, but this time it wasn't meant as an invitation. He simply smiled out of pure happiness of having Maria next to him in his lovely old Volvo the same way he so many times in the past had her in the back seat of his Plymouth Barracuda. He glanced over to Maria who smiled back at him.

Maria had that very Italian look - her roots were only one generation back in Perugia in the district of Umbria. Her mother had moved to New York after falling in love with a returning American soldier who came back to visit the area he had fought in during the war. She decided, in an instant, to move to the U.S. with him.

Five tumultuous years later, they were divorced but not before the birth of Maria in 1958. As the sole provider she needed an income to support herself and her only child. Since her ex-husband came from nearby Peekskill, where they had lived with her in-laws since coming over from Italy, she had visited Cold Spring many times and had fallen in love with the village. A perfect place to open up her café and to live upstairs in the building she was able to buy with money her in-laws graciously lent her. They had always supported her and even more so now when she was the mother of their first and only grandchild.

The tiny, but extremely well-shaped body of a five foot two Italian beauty was only one of the attributes Harry liked about Maria. Her hair, no gray traces whatsoever thanks to a constant race with time. Though colored dark brown for the last couple of years, it was still as silky and shiny as he remembered it being back then.

Her very animated way of getting her opinion across, using not only her voice but her whole body to speak was a very charming contrast to his reserved and careful way of communicating; no doubt a testament to his Swedish heritage. Maria appreciated his thoughtfulness of not speaking out until he had thought through what he was about to say.

Harry's mind wasn't entirely on the road and he had to quickly maneuver over to the right lane after being halfway over on the other side of the road.

"Oh, I'm sorry Maria. My mind was wandering off for a quick second."

"And I didn't even touch you." Maria laughed, smiled and quickly leaned over to place another quick kiss on his cheek.

Taking a quick glance over to Maria, catching her blue eyes, full sexy lips, very sparing and neutral make-up, he took a mental picture of her. When adding the slightly pointy nose, her slender, inviting body with breasts that when touched were warm and inviting like a bird nest in the spring, he knew she had everything a man could desire in a woman. Plus the one thing that made Maria the special one - she was and had continued to be his best friend over all these years, of all the people who wandered in and out of his life.

His guy friends were few, probably because he was never around long enough to experience the typical male bonding activities like going to sporting events together, fishing trips or having a beer at the local pub watching Monday night football. Instead Harry always seemed to be on the run. Maybe running away from what he saw as a stale and boring every day, repetitious lifestyle. He preferred the adventurous, unpredictable, and exciting life of exploring new places, new people, and new cultures.

But today, he was reminded why Maria once more was sitting next to him. It made him happy to feel like he at last could settle down emotionally with a woman and he was looking forward to see where their journey would take them. He smiled, leaned over and reciprocated Maria's earlier kiss with a quick kiss on her beautiful and inviting lips, making him wish they could skip dinner and make love in the back of his Volvo, like the teenagers they once were back in his Plymouth Barracuda.

But first he was very much looking forward to dinner with Maria and to share the photograph with her - like best friends do.

Chapter Seven

After parking the car they took a moment to view the moon and stars glittering over the Hudson River in the chilly but not cold early April evening. All the snow was gone and the evening had that fresh air of a new beginning. Harry and Maria were holding hands while walking towards the restaurant. Maria was mindfully aware of her situation as a married woman but could care less knowing it was only a matter of time before she was going to free herself from years of, what she now considered, a prison term. Harry enjoyed the attention and tonight was of course special because the woman next to him was Maria. And he surprised himself by thinking and hoping that this was the beginning of many more days and nights of taking Maria to restaurants, on trips and adventures.

"Welcome to The Half Moon," the manager greeted them with a warm smile. "I have a window table for two as requested. Just follow me please."

Harry with a hand gesture let Maria take the lead. She smiled at him and her facial expression left no one in doubt. She was not just happy. She was ecstatic. She gladly followed the manager, passing the raging fireplace which sent warm feelings down her spine and goose bumps all over her bare arms and legs. When passing the dining guests already engaged in conversation and meals, she couldn't avoid noticing how they looked up and scanned the two of them as if to acknowledge their presence.

Maria knew many people from the river towns along the Hudson, yet the thought of anyone recognizing either of them, never occurred to her. Her mind was made up. She was determined to make Harry a happy man, making sure he never had to doubt the risk he felt he was taking by committing with such passion. Moving along on a path with so many possibilities, side roads to explore, with no dead ends in sight, was what she saw coming.

Harry had caught up to her and was right behind her when the manager stopped and with an elegant move seated them at the best table in the restaurant right by the end of the newly added extension. This placed them as close to the water as possible with a gorgeous view of the Tappan Zee Bridge on Maria's right and an equally beautiful view of New York City on her left. Once Maria had been seated Harry leaned over and placed a gentle kiss right below her left ear. The spot that always sent those warm feelings and goose bumps Maria had just experienced when passing by the fire place.

Looking up and into Harry's friendly eyes she smiled and thought to herself that the fire sparking inside Harry, so sudden but oh so welcome, was a fire she would feed and keep alive.

"Is this ok, Maria?" he whispered after placing the kiss.

Is this ok he says, Maria thought to herself, wondering if Harry had lost his mind. Of course it's ok -

it's more than ok but she controlled her feelings and smiled.

"It's wonderful," she whispered.

Harry took his seat. The sun had already set and the moon and stars were casting their light on the dark and somewhat mysterious waters of the Hudson River. Seated and looking across the table at Maria he realized he may have reached a crossroads in his life with multiple possibilities of finding new exciting things to explore. Not alone as he had grown accustomed to for so many years, but together with a woman he felt so comfortable around. At a place as serene as this, with the eternal lights of New York burning as a symbol of the life and competitive spirit of the city, as opposed to the much more quite northern upstream part of the Hudson. They were right in between the two worlds they both desired and felt comfortable balancing and living in.

The menus were brought to the table and the specials were read by a waitress named Yvette who literally smiled with her whole face. Maria and Harry paid scant attention to her, or the specials. This was an evening when food was secondary. Of primary importance was them being together in this lovely setting. They casually looked over the menu when Harry broke the silence that had followed after the smiling waitress had left them to decide.

"So, there's a first for everything," he said while reaching out touching Maria's hand.

"Yes, there certainly is but we can't really claim that we are virgins at this." Maria filled in thinking Harry was talking about them, since he reached out to touch her hand.

Harry laughed. "Well, I meant this is the first time we've dined here." He moved his hand away. Maria reached out after it and grabbed it again.

"Oh no, you won't get off that easily." She smiled while looking him straight in the eyes. She wanted to find out more about him by reaching deeper inside Harry than he had ever allowed anyone to do before.

Maria had been hurt and gotten over it, only to see her feelings rekindle when Harry arrived back, last year, to settle down for good, in Cold Spring, between his travels and adventures. Harry had come to her café to casually announce his return, and that he had purchased a nice one bedroom apartment down by the harbor across from The Hudson House River Inn. Her life had once more been rocked to its foundation. All the old emotions stirred up, hopes rekindled and the waiting game begun. Every time he walked in to get his morning latte, spoke to her, looked at her, she made sure that he knew that she was available. Not rushing anything but making sure he read, understood and received her signals.

"Hmm, I like that." Harry said with his usual smooth voice but this time with an undertone of sincerity that Maria caught right away. She playfully started to touch his leg under the table with her right foot so as to confirm she had read the signal correctly. Harry did nothing to stop her. On the contrary he squeezed her hand harder and if it wouldn't have been for the smiling waitress returning to ask them if they had decided on something to drink, they may have decided to leave right then.

"Excuse me for interrupting," she said with sweetness in her voice that really caught Harry off guard. He couldn't avoid moving his eyes from Maria's face to the waitress who had this picture perfect smile as if she had no worries at all, completely focused on making sure her guests were taken care of and left happily, presumably with a big tip.

"Would you care for something to drink Ma'am?" she asked Maria, looking directly at her, fully aware of her charm and youth and the fact that you never let a customer even remotely flirt with you in the company of another woman.

"I would love a glass of Chianti," she answered while unintentionally releasing her hand from Harry's.

"And for you Sir?" she asked turning her smiling face to Harry.

"I'd like a glass of Chardonnay please," Harry replied before realizing he was driving. Well, I'm sure one glass is ok. This romantic dinner calls for at least a glass of wine this early in the evening he thought to himself while quickly turning his eyes and attention back to Maria. This time he gently touched her hand, playing with her fingers in an almost nervous way. Harry knew this was different.

61

Tonight it wasn't the woman sitting across from him who showed anxiety and tension. It was he, who for the first time felt that tingly nervousness of performance anxiety.

Maria raised her left hand from under the table to grab the menu when she accidentally ripped the paper table cover the restaurant had placed over the clean, white and beautiful table cloth.

Harry immediately raised his hand to get the attention of the pretty smiling waitress Yvette. She noticed Harry's hand and acknowledged with a nod that she was going to be right over.

"Do you have a question Sir?"

"Not exactly, but I wonder if you could be kind enough and have the paper table cover removed? We would much rather dine without getting paper cuts." Harry tried, as always, not to make too big of a deal out of things but he did think it was rather tacky at a fine restaurant to be treated like children unable to keep their food on their plate or mouth.

"Not a problem." "I'll have a staff member come over and take it off."

It's funny but they never call them busboys anymore; Harry thought.

"Thanks Yvette. I really appreciate it." Harry thought he rather successfully had defused the situation without embarrassing anyone. He did though decide to call the manager the next day to let him know that a restaurant of their standard should consider dropping their paper covers, at least for the evening dinner sitting.

"Where were we Maria?"

While looking over the menu Maria continued to playfully touch Harry's legs under the table with her right foot. The recessed lighting right above their table cast a spotlight like warm beam of light on Maria. Harry enjoyed the scenery. She looks gorgeous he thought to himself. Maria smiled, knowing exactly what Harry thought, loving the attention.

"I'll have the sea bass," she said after taking just a quick look at the menu. "It sounds delicious." "And you Harry? What are you having?"

"I'll have the NY Strip Steak;" Harry replied in a rush since he didn't want to dwell on the details of all the options on the menu now when Maria had made a quick decision and was ready to continue their conversation.

His knowledge of wine was limited to knowing that red wine normally goes better with meat and white wine with fish. So he knew he had made a faux pas by ordering the one and only glass of wine he could have for the night - at least until they were safely back in Cold Spring. But Chardonnay was definitely his favorite wine so let me defy the traditions and have the wine I prefer with the food I prefer, regardless of "rules" he thought to himself.

Maria raised her glass but suddenly started looking over Harry's shoulder like she was toasting the couple sitting right behind Harry. Maria was still looking at the couple when Harry picked up his glass, turned around and took a curious look at the couple.

Maria leaned over and said in a low voice "I was looking at the man holding his wine glass." "Did you see?"

Harry had noticed the same thing and he recalled the story his mom had told him about his dad and how he used to do the same thing when toasting his family and friends at dinners. It was apparently a Swedish thing. The proposer of the toast engages the eye of the person being toasted, and "skål" is said. A slight bow of the head, and a twinkle of the eye - and a sip of the wine is taken. Just before the glass is put back on the table, the eyes meet again and there is another friendly nod.

"Let me show you how to do it." He smiled, lifted his glass and Maria followed his move. He looked her in the eye, said "skål", bowed ever so gently with his head and with a twinkle of the eye took a sip of the Chardonnay and she of her Chianti, lowered the glass and exchanged eye contact once more before putting back the glass on the table.

They both laughed and with the laugh they released any remaining nervousness or anxiety they had felt about meeting for dinner after reconnecting only one day earlier.

The rest of the dinner they spent catching up on old memories. For dessert Maria's sweet tooth had chosen the chocolate volcano, a moist chocolate cake filled with warm ganache. Harry preferred the more traditional New York cheesecake with fresh mixed berries and vanilla sauce.

He decided it was time to bring up the photograph.

"How is your chocolate cake, Maria?" Harry asked while leaning over to steal a piece.

"It's divine. Maria laughed and took a piece of Harry's cheesecake. "Hmm, not bad," she said.

Harry took out the picture from his jacket pocket and put it next to Maria's cake plate. She was surprised and startled for a moment and pushed herself away from the table as if to protect herself.

"What is this Harry?" she asked after collecting her thoughts.

"I don't know," Harry answered looking at Maria to see her reaction.

"What do you mean, you don't know"?

"Well, I found it at Joe's in one of his old postcard boxes the other day and it seems to have a very interesting story to it. I think I may want to try and find out what it is."

Maria took a quick look at the picture and started to wonder if the sudden but wonderful reunion with Harry was going to come to an abrupt end. Is he leaving on one of his trips again she thought to herself? Her eyes moved from the photo in front of her to Harry who was looking straight at her.

"I know," he said without waiting for Maria's reaction. "It's old and the writing on the back is rather interesting, isn't it?"

Maria moved her eyes back to the picture. She started to tear up and Harry noticed something wasn't right.

"Maria, are you alright? I hope the picture didn't upset you in any way," he apologetically said with a concerned voice.

Maria looked up again.

"No, no, I'm alright," she replied and smiled. She again moved her eyes down to the picture, started scanning it, upset that she let her feelings show.

"On the back of the picture there is a date. It looks like they arrived somewhere, presumably here, after the war ended in 1945," Harry filled in.

Maria, now intrigued by the picture, had forgotten all about her emotional reaction to Harry's mention of another possible adventure trip. She instead looked at it with a puzzled expression on her face. Harry, noticing the change, started to wonder if bringing up the photograph when the evening had been going so well up to this point was such a good idea after all. He regretted doing so and moved his hand over to grab the photograph.

"No." Maria put her hand over Harry's to prevent him from taking it. "There is something familiar with this picture but I can't figure out what it is," she said with a puzzled expression. "I think I have seen this photo before," she finally said.

Now it was Harry's turn to look puzzled.

"I'm sure you will eventually remember if you have seen it previously."

On their way back to Cold Spring there was no mention of the photo. Instead their conversation circled back to the evening and how great a time they both had. It was as if they just started where they had left off. Maria placed her hand on Harry's right hand, touching him ever so gently not to distract him from focusing on the road ahead. She had made up her mind. If Harry was going to ask her to stay for the night she would. She would just leave a note for her husband, if by any remote chance he showed up. He hadn't for the last two weeks and she didn't even know where he was. Wondering why even leave a note for someone who didn't care to tell her what he was up to, made her even more determined to spend the night with the one person who did care.

Her daughters, Francesca and Serafina, both married but with no grandchildren yet, lived nearby—one in Garrison and the other in Wappinger Falls. There was no love lost concerning their father who they blamed for messing up their lives as teenagers with his drug use and bad influence. Now adults and drug free themselves they appreciated even more the sacrifices their mother had made, being there for them when times were tough.

Their grandmother had told them how it was for her to be a single parent, running the café and taking care of Maria at the same time. She had also told them things about their dad that Maria had never revealed. She had done so not to turn them against him, but for them to understand the dangers with drugs and what it can do to a person, a relationship, a family. She didn't really know much about drugs but she knew what it did to her grandchildren's dad and how miserable and unhappy it made their mom.

Maria's daughters had a very close relationship with their grandmother and when she passed they told Maria everything their grandmother had told them over the years. It made Maria happy, sad and angry at the same time. But overall she was grateful that her mother had spoken to them, and been there for her grandchildren, during their tough years as they grew. It had also, in a way, strengthened the bond between her children, knowing that there were no secrets between them. Her daughters had over the years encouraged Maria to divorce their father or at least go out and enjoy her life. Meet a man that could make her happy instead of being left behind by a man who obviously didn't care if she was there or not.

Maria had found her man and she wasn't going to let him disappear.

She wrote the note, picked up some overnight things and spent the night with Harry.

Chapter Eight

The early morning sun broke through the blinds like sharp beams. Maria woke up, turned around only to see an empty spot next to her. The smell of freshly brewed coffee and scrambled eggs convinced her that yesterday wasn't just a dream, but a wonderful and romantic reality. She took a deep inhale through her nose to take it all in. The smell of Harry, the unmistakable smell of her "April Aromatics Nectar of Love" - her favorite very sensual, deep and rich perfume - a luxury she would only allow herself now that Harry was around.

Last night was certainly an occasion to wear something special. She grabbed the sheet, smelled the sex, smiled and whispered ever so gently "I love this guy," when Harry entered the bedroom with a tray of two espressos, scrambled eggs with toast and two glasses of freshly squeezed orange juice. Oh yes, this man is a keeper, that's for sure she thought to herself when sitting up to receive the tray. Harry leaned over and kissed her.

"Good morning my Pearl," he said and smiled.

"I haven't heard you say that since High School." She blushed. It was one of those teenage greetings Harry always used. He varied them, finding new ways of naming Maria. All in an effort to never have to say "my love", something Harry throughout his adult life never had said to any woman.

Pearl was the most beautiful name he gave me, Maria thought while taking a first sip of espresso. Harry decided to lie down next to her, watch her drink her espresso while gently moving his hand under the sheet, finding the warm and soft legs of Maria's naked body.

Maria gasped, smiled and closed her eyes letting Harry's hand move freely up her inner thigh, lightly and gently finding his way up.

"Oh, Harry," she moaned moving her head back and having a very hard time resisting what ultimately would follow if she allowed him to continue. She finally got the strength to break the love spell and as gently as Harry had moved his hand up her thigh, grabbed his hand and moved it ever so reluctantly away.

"I need to get ready to open up the café in half an hour," she whispered.

They finished their breakfast quickly, took a shower together more to save time than anything else. Both, in many ways practical people, had their minds on getting on with their day and avoiding Mrs. Rose. A rumor about Maria's whereabouts last night wasn't something the two of them wanted to plant in Mrs. Rose's mind when she arrived for her first cup of coffee, less than 15 minutes hence.

It had turned into a fixation for her to be the first customer in the morning. It all came down to making sure she didn't miss anything that potentially could turn into the gossip of the day. As they head out from Harry's flat, they exchanged a quick but romantic kiss and Harry looked outside to make sure no one was passing by his apartment. They, in all honesty, could not care less but Maria thought it was better not to advertise their romance to the village gossip queen Mrs. Rose until such time Maria had the chance to tell her husband that she was leaving him.

This thought only occurred to Maria, but she knew that the time had come for her to make the move regardless of how Harry would react. She knew Harry had not been interested in settling down for any extended period of time but she also knew she wasn't just any woman. She was Maria, Harry's first love. She felt she had nothing to lose at this point in going after him with all her soul. Leaving her husband after all these years of suffering and hesitating was a decision everyone around her knew was coming. Not even Mrs. Rose could turn her divorce into a scandal.

"Good morning, Mrs. Rose," Maria greeted her as she was standing outside the café wondering why it wasn't open yet and why Maria didn't come to the door after she knocked on it, not once but a few times.

"Good morning Maria." "What a wonderful morning we have," she said while scanning Maria from top to toe. "I was just wondering if my watch needed a new battery," she sarcastically commented, referring to Maria's late arrival.

"No, no Mrs. Rose. I'm sorry for being a couple of minutes late. I was tied up with something this morning," Maria replied to her in a polite voice.

"Yes I figured as much when I saw you coming up from the other side of the railway station. Had some business down the harbor this morning?" she asked in a probing voice.

Maria didn't know how to respond, so she simply answered with a yes while digging through her bag to find her keys to unlock and open the café door for Mrs. Rose.

"It's certainly a beautiful morning for a stroll down by the river," Mrs. Rose continued, determined to find out exactly what Maria's business was all about.

"Yes Mrs. Rose. I suggest you bring your coffee with you down to the gazebo this wonderful morning. Maybe you will catch a glimpse of something or someone down there by the water front," Maria replied in a sharp irritated tone that even startled Mrs. Rose who sat down at one of the small tables. While waiting for Maria to start up her coffee machine and prepare the first cup of coffee for the day, no more words were spoken.

Maria smiled. Not only did she have a wonderful dinner last evening and an even better night but she had also successfully silenced Mrs. Rose and her investigative mind, at least for the moment. That was enough for Maria, who just wanted to hang on to the wonderful feeling of waking up not alone, but with Harry serving her breakfast in bed. Yes, it's turning out to be a wonderful morning, she thought, just like Mrs. Rose had said.

Harry ended up being her second customer of the day. He said goodbye to Mrs. Rose who was just leaving. Upon exiting she gave him a look of disapproval as she glanced over to Maria to catch her reaction to Harry. He got his latte with heart shaped foam on top and stole a kiss just as Mrs. Rose turned around and before Joe of all people entered.

"Good morning, Joe," Maria said, surprised to see him since he seldom left his house and store.

"What brings you out from your dungeon?" Harry asked with a laugh before Joe even got a chance to say good morning.

"Good morning to you too, Harry," he said and added, "Thank you for ordering a latte for me." He quickly grabbed Harry's latte from the counter before Harry got a chance to react. He took a quick sip, not noticing the heart shaped foam, before putting it back down. He laughed and felt better than he had in a long time. Knowing Harry he thought he would stop by his place to follow up on the investigation he assumed Harry already was in the middle of. Locating the people in the picture was for rather obvious reasons top priority for him. The sooner he could leave his unfortunate renewed contact with Frank behind him the better. At the same time there was something that triggered a desire to revisit a period of his life that had left him flush broke, an addict and in prison. It was a rollercoaster life of highs and lows; women; money; drugs and victims along his path of destruction. But it was a damn good time and much more exciting than the small town boring lifestyle he lived now. Not that he wanted the old life back, but he wanted to feel useful and having Harry do the legwork for him also appealed to him.

"I was actually on my way over to you," he said turning to Harry and tilting his head back to stare at the over six foot man in front of him, "when I saw you in here."

"Let's walk down to the harbor." Harry grabbed his latte from the counter, gave Maria a nod and a wink with his left eye as if he was toasting her with a "skål" and left the café with Joe, who struggled to keep up with Harry's fast pace walk.

"Did you get a chance to start looking for the family in the picture?" Joe asked, out of breath.

"No, you only gave it to me yesterday, Joe. You have to give me a little bit more time than that," Harry replied laughing. "Since when did you get things done in a hurry, my friend?" He jabbed at Joe who avoided the friendly jab by instinctively taking a couple of steps back. I haven't lost my touch, he thought to himself.

"You need to work on that jab, Harry."

They reached the river front and sat down on one of the benches.

"Did Frank tell you anything else?" "He must have given you a little bit more to go on than just a picture?"

"Not really, Harry. But he did mention that he thought the family was from Umbria."

"Well that's a start."

Harry knew the area rather well after spending a travel magazine photography assignment in Perugia, the capital of Umbria, a couple of years ago. He remembered what Maria had told him last night. She had possibly recognized the picture. Wasn't her mother from Perugia?

Harry got excited. He had his first clue and Maria may play a more important role in finding the family than he ever imagined when deciding to show her the picture last night.

Chapter Nine

Maria's day passed by quickly and she was relieved when she left and locked the door of the café behind her. She, for obvious reasons, hadn't slept much the night before. A bath, a glass of wine and a relaxing evening with a good book was what she was looking forward to. Her house on Fair Street was a short walk from her café. She decided to call Harry who picked up after only one ring.

"Hi Maria, done for the day?" he started off saying even before she had a chance to say hello.

"Yes, just left the café and on my way home I wanted to call and thank you for a wonderful evening" she said with the voice of a very satisfied woman.

"Not sure you need to thank me. I'm as grateful to you for a wonderful evening and night." Harry thought back to when they, last night, naked and entangled in a passion, had recalled that close to 40 years had passed. Feeling as young and vibrant as they'd ever felt they had reached an explosive orgasm with him sitting on his reading chair, Maria on top of him, both moving rhythmically like two artists singing a duet in perfect harmony.

Harry woke up from his daydreaming when Maria, on the spur of the moment said: "I was hoping I could see you this coming Saturday," without having planned to. Even worse, having no idea what she had in mind for them, or who should be running the café if she took a day off.

"I'd love that Maria but who is going to take care of the café?" Harry read her mind.

"Not sure yet, I'll figure something out. Maybe we could take a hike up to Breakneck Ridge, like in the old days?" Maria filled in to make sure Harry wouldn't find a reason to say no because the plans weren't set in stone.

"Sounds great," Harry replied and continued "What are your plans for tonight?"

"A bath, a glass wine and a good book," Maria again seductively whispered her reply.

"Wish I could join you for a glass," Harry said and added "and in the bath that is."

Without replying but smiling and laughing ever so gently into the phone she simply said:

"Tonight isn't the night for you and me - it's "Maria time."

Little did Maria know that her evening wasn't going to be anything like what she had planned.

When she turned onto Fair Street from Main she spotted Robert's car in the distance outside her house. Robert was her husband whom she hadn't seen in over two weeks. Why tonight, she thought angrily to herself when stepping onto her wraparound porch, opening the unlocked door and entering only to see Robert in the kitchen. He was drinking a glass of wine from the open bottle she had been looking forward to drinking by herself, without company from anyone, especially not Robert.

"Maria," Robert growled at her with a grin and the slurred speech of someone who had been drinking one too many already.

God knows what other drugs he was on she thought.

"Robert, what do you want? You haven't showed up in over two weeks and hardly ever for the last six months. Now suddenly you are standing here acting like you never left."

Maria, calm and collected, thought it was best not to overreact while at the same time making sure Robert didn't think he could just come and go as he pleases anymore.

"What do I want?" he in a surprised and angry voice replied, attempting to take a step forward towards Maria who by now was only a couple of feet away from him. He stumbled and had to grab onto the corner of the kitchen counter to avoid falling.

"Robert, you're drunk AND high, please leave." Maria looked straight at Robert whose eyes and face were far from friendly at this point.

"I want to fuck you," he screamed and made another attempt to get to Maria, this time he successfully grabbed her left arm with his left hand, turning his body in a desperate attempt to grab her throat with his right hand. Maria, shocked and stunned by Robert's aggressive attempt to force himself on her, stood like a frozen statue unable to move.

As Robert's right hand moved towards Maria's throat she did nothing to protect herself. She was terrified, stunned and in shock. The memories of Robert, before drugs and alcohol planted a demon inside his body, mind and soul, flashed in front of her eyes like a silent movie. The memories were futile of their happy first couple of years when their children were born and they both worked hard to support a family of four, Maria helping her mother at the café and Robert as a car salesperson. Then Robert stopped caring and instead just became a victim of heroin and alcohol addiction. Year after year of an on and off switch of addictions, affairs and jobs he never could hold onto for long. Suddenly he left for what Maria at the time hoped was for good.

But he always came back, begging for forgiveness with promises of becoming a better person. It only lasted a couple of months or sometimes, weeks. Occasionally, he stuck around longer but always ended up on the heroin track; a track the kids traveled on as his passengers during some very bad and tough teenage years.

Maria, meanwhile, struggled to keep up with the café and her business degree night classes. It was then the kids' grandmother came to their rescue, Robert knew better than to occasionally show up. Most of the time he was sober and drug free for a day or two while visiting his daughters before leaving as suddenly as he had appeared at the doorstep.

Robert's right hand turned into a fist and the sound of it landing on Maria's lips and left cheek gave the silent movie an unwanted sound effect; the sound of the impact and the smell and taste of blood in Maria's mouth.

It happened so fast and without warning. Robert had never struck Maria or the kids before. There was no time, no reason for her to even remotely think she would have to protect herself from him.

Now the evidence was in the blood and the painfully battered face of Maria as she stumbled back. At about the same time Robert fell on the floor, got up, spitting, screaming and shouting at her:

"Come here bitch," he slurred in a rage. He again raised his arm; his right fist locked for yet another blow to Maria's face. She instinctively, and to protect herself from falling, grabbed on to a kitchen cabinet drawer behind her. She felt something and without realizing what she was holding in her right hand, raised her arm to ward off the next blow from the man she once loved and thought she knew.

Robert didn't make any sound when the bread knife punctured his shoulder. His eyes opened wide in disbelief, turning his head towards the point where the blood was slowly, but steadily pulsating through his white shirt into a red mess.

"Shit." He stared at Maria, holding the right hand that had struck Maria's face on his left shoulder in an attempt to stem the blood.

Maria froze like a statue. She couldn't move. They both stared at each other without saying a word. When she thought Robert was going to strike her again, he turned around, rushed out on the porch leaving a trail of blood behind him, staggered into his car and sped off.

Maria kneeled down on the kitchen floor, holding the palms of her hands on the, bloody and slippery floor before her. Tears streamed down her face. She could taste the blood from the gash on her cheek and the split in her swollen lips. She started to shake and cry uncontrollably.

Harry had just left his apartment to get a bite to eat when a car came speeding onto Main Street from Fair Street, turning east and then onto route 9D, heading north. This was far from an everyday event in the small, sleepy town of Cold Spring. Harry couldn't remember ever seeing a car turn so fast and furious and speeding up on Main Street.

Nothing but silence followed. There was no chase; no police following the car. Harry got an uneasy feeling that something was terribly wrong. Fair Street - that's where Maria lives he thought to himself while half running turned around the corner to her house 200 feet from Main Street.

He stopped right in front of her house. With an expression of fear and desperation he stood there as if he couldn't believe what he was seeing. Leading up to her house were red traces of blood. He quickly ran up and onto the porch almost slipping on the thick gooey blood on the stairs.

"Maria," he screamed. Expecting the worst, he ran into the house, the adrenalin pumping, his face drained of color. He found her lying on the kitchen floor in a pool of blood. Wrapping his arms around her the only thing he kept saying was "Maria, talk to me. Are you alright?" in between her hysterical cries and tears. Maria's hands tightly squeezed Harry's arms, not letting go even when he tried to loosen the grip to take a look at her face. The blood on her hands, now transferred to Harry's white polo shirt and arms, was the only thing he could see. He gently moved her forward to a sitting position and loosened the frantic grip on his arms. He stared into her beaten and bloody face in horror.

"Oh my God, Maria." "What happened?" he asked, without expecting an answer. "Who did this to you?"

Chapter Ten

"Ah Hell," Robert screamed out loud, moving across from right to left on Route 9N at 65 miles per hour. It just started to sink in. Maria had stabbed him with force he never thought would come from her. It wasn't until now he started to feel the pain. Finding it difficult to breathe, he panicked. He held the steering wheel with his right hand, his left arm hanging and useless with blood streaming down from his wound. He looked down at his left hand to see if he could move it up to grab the steering wheel. The only thing he saw was a hand looking like it was wearing a dark red glove, fingers and a lifeless hand--a reminder of how useless his life had been. It was the pain that blurred his vision and made his head spin.

He didn't hear or see it coming. Why should he? He had lived his whole life lying to himself, friends, his daughters and family. All he had done over the past 30 years was to lie and cheat to yet another high, getting enough money to support not his family but his drug habit. His whole life was about denial, avoiding reality at all costs.

He didn't hear or see it coming.

He was losing consciousness and the only thing he envisioned was Maria's beaten face. Why did I do that to her, he thought, when he felt the first impact? He saw Maria's arm raised. Was it her fist landing a blow to my face? Where did she get all that strength from?

That was when the car smashed into a huge oak on the side of the road. His face hit the shattered windshield and literally split in half as a huge tree branch broke through the car. The bread knife had sliced him like he was a loaf of bread, but the pain of the impact was excruciating. The flesh, blood, and unrecognizable pieces of his face splashed all over what was left of the front of the car. A tree branch had basically impaled him; entering right under his cheek bone, slicing his tongue and exiting where his left eye ball used to be.

Next hit was to his groin area. The tree trunk had sliced the car right about in half and his groin was just in the way. His right leg was cut off and the blood still left found another way to escape, leaving him white and cold but still alive. He should have been dead by then, but there was something or someone keeping him alive.

He moved his head down and with the only eye he had left he saw the big open hole where his leg had once been attached to his hip. He looked up again and as he was staring in the rearview mirror, he saw what had become of him. A loser, no good for anything that deserved the pain and misery left before death would liberate him.

The car came to a stop and while the gasoline poured over his body, engine still miraculously running, he felt the explosion rip off the left side of his body, leaving what was left of him to burn. The last thing he would feel was the pain from his own burning flesh. He would not hurt Maria or his family ever again.

Chapter Eleven

Maria, now calm, stared down at the kitchen floor, still in shock. Harry had moved her away from the pool of blood but she was still in the room where Robert had attacked her. Harry was just about to call for help when a voice outside on the porch shouted:

"This is the police. – is everything ok?"

Harry put down his phone, wondering how the police could arrive even before he had a chance to make the call.

"We are in the kitchen." Harry was happy to see Officer James Flynn. He had known him for many years and when Harry moved back, Officer Flynn or Jim had looked him up to welcome him back to town and Harry had invited him in for a glass of whiskey. Before they knew it the bottle was empty.

A lot was shared that night and Jim got a first glimpse into Harry's private life– something very few people were privileged to learn. As part of the Cold Spring Town Police effort to save money and limit the number of cars they were using, Officer Flynn had been assigned one of the two bikes approved in last year's budget. He had been out on his evening patrol when he passed by Maria's house and noticed the blood on the pavement leading up to her porch and front door. Officer Flynn was, like the rest of town, aware of Maria's abusive husband, and wasn't surprised, although shocked, at what he saw when he entered the kitchen, carefully avoiding the blood. He could only guess that Robert had a hand in this. Jim had already radioed in and Harry and Maria could hear the sirens outside.

"Let me take a look at you Maria," he said, gently pushing Harry away.

"Did Robert do this to you? Maria nodded. Officer Flynn turned to Harry to ask him what he was doing here but before he got a chance, Harry told him he was walking up Main Street for a bite to eat when he saw a car turning from Fair Street east onto Main Street at a very high speed. Instinctively Harry turned onto Fair Street and started to run up towards Maria's house.

Officer Flynn looked around, before turning to Maria again.

He looked down at her. He couldn't find any wounds other than those on her beaten face, cracked cheek and lips, none of which could have caused all this blood loss.

"Did he have any sort of weapon he threatened you with? Or, did you defend yourself with one?"

"I don't know. He lunged towards me and suddenly there was blood everywhere."

Maria tried to keep it together but she felt scared and couldn't really remember exactly what had happened. Harry put his arms around her to calm her down and looked at Officer Flynn with a plea to stop the questioning for now until she had a chance to calm down and get medical treatment.

One of the police cars arriving at the scene was instructed by Officer Flynn to go into pursuit on 9N after Harry told him about the perpetrator's escape route. The ambulance arrived shortly thereafter and Maria walked toward it with Harry holding a steady grip around her, but Maria could not stop shaking.

"She needs a blanket," Harry said turning to one of the volunteer EMS workers without hesitation. "She's in shock."

He didn't recognize the med tech. Must be one of the new ones, he thought. He glanced over to ask for her name but thought better of his aggressive actions.

"Harry, stay behind, I've got a few questions for you," Officer Flynn shouted when Maria was ready to be taken to the local hospital in the ambulance that had just arrived.

"I'll be right over when I'm done with Officer Flynn," Harry said to Maria. He reluctantly returned to the house. The other officers had started to seal off the area.

"What did you see when entering the house?" asked Flynn.

"Nothing except Maria on her knees, hands covered in the blood on the floor in front of her."

"Did you see who was in the car?"

"No. Only that it was a man driving, everything happened so fast and then he sped off going east on Main Street before turning onto route 9 going north."

"Maria said it was Robert. Do you know Robert?"

"No," replied Harry. "I can't say I do. Only know about him and his problems. He hardly showed up here anymore and when he did it was always to ask for some money from Maria or their daughters. I think Maria was going to ask him for a divorce. The marriage was over a long time ago."

Harry regretted adding the last part. He didn't really know and could only guess. It didn't' seem right to mention her divorce with what he assumed was Roberts' blood on the kitchen floor. What took place here he wondered to himself while looking down on all the blood?

"Harry, regarding your relationship with Maria," Officer Flynn leaned over and whispered so that the other officers wouldn't hear him. "Did Robert know?" Harry had of course mentioned his high school sweetheart and the rekindled feelings for her over the bottle of whiskey last month.

"No, I know Maria didn't say anything to him about our High School relationship. Why should she? It was way before he came into the picture." Harry replied in an offhanded way, thinking he should have kept his life private at the time the whiskey did the talking.

"But what about just recently? Officer Flynn continued with no intention of changing the topic.

"What do you mean, Jim"? Harry used his first name in an attempt to keep it off the record and between the two of them.

"Well, you know, it was rather obvious for most of the folks here in the village that you and Maria had something going on since you arrived back in town."

How ironic it is, Harry thought, that nothing more than a flirtation had been going on between the two of them until only a couple of days ago. Obviously Mrs. Rose had been spreading rumors for quite some time now. And Jim had apparently remembered their conversation despite all the whiskey.

"You'll have to ask Maria but like I said, Robert certainly didn't know about our high school relationship and very unlikely anything about my personal life or flirtation with Maria. Again, how could he? He's only been back a couple of times for one or two days since then." Harry answered in a curt way.

"Yes I'll ask Maria."

Jim looked at Harry as if to say I don't judge you, just want to have all facts straight. He had a pretty good idea what had taken place here earlier. He wanted to do his job, leaving nothing behind that could jeopardize his report that this was a case of a domestic dispute turned violent.

He looked down on the floor and right under the dishwasher, partially hidden under it, was a knife. He put some gloves on – something he had forgotten to do when entering the crime scene earlier – and picked it up. It was a bread knife with a lot of blood on it. Putting it into a plastic bag, marking it crime scene evidence #1, he looked up at Harry and said, still whispering:

"I won't find your finger prints on this knife will I?"

Harry looked at him with a stern and surprised facial expression.

"No, you won't," Harry quickly replied.

"I didn't think I would," Jim leaned over even closer to Harry before whispering his reply.

"I should be able to close this investigation after speaking to Maria later tonight and once we apprehend Robert," he said. Officer Flynn didn't want this to drag on for too long. He knew Maria and respected her for what she had accomplished and gone through in her life with Robert, who he, like the rest of the village, despised. Harry was the kind of guy who obviously could, and was physically capable of hurting Robert because of his relationship with Maria. But after sharing a bottle of whisky back then when Harry moved back, Jim was sure that the story Harry told was the truth and he saw no reason to doubt it.

On his way out he told the officer outside to keep anyone from entering until they had secured the crime scene and apprehended Maria's husband and probable perpetrator.

Chapter Twelve

Harry arrived at Maria's bedside wearing a clean shirt and pants. Maria's face and lips were swollen and the doctors had already glued the wound on her cheek instead of using conventional stitches. Harry was happy with their choice. The less she had to be reminded of this incident the better and a scar would bring back the bad memories every time she looked at herself in the mirror.

"How are you feeling?" Harry leaned over and kissed her gently on her right cheek.

"I'm ok, Harry. Thank you for stopping by. You didn't really have to," she replied, attempting a smile, but the pain reminded her about what had happened less than two hours before.

"I just spoke to Jim." Maria seemed relieved and Harry didn't want to probe into the incident more than necessary. It was rather obvious to him what had happened and once Robert was apprehended he would talk to Maria about getting a restraining order, a good divorce lawyer and some time off.

For now he wanted to make sure Maria was getting all the help she required to leave her past behind and to start over. His feelings for her were obviously strong and they told him it was the right thing to do. He wanted to make sure he did everything possible to protect her. He knew what needed to be done. Maria, battered, emotionally abused and despite the pain, a very beautiful woman, was lying in front of him in a hospital bed. He felt guilty because he hadn't had the guts to ask her to be at his side earlier.

"I'm just very upset that I didn't realize earlier how dangerous Robert was. And how unhealthy my relationship with him had become." Maria looked straight at Harry seeming to have read his mind and concern. "I'm glad you realize that."

Harry, while looking into her tearful blue eyes, added:

"And of course I'll be there to help you. How about I get in touch with my attorney? She does divorce cases as well…" Harry hesitated bringing it up but felt Maria had initiated it by acknowledging how unhealthy her relationship with Robert had been.

"Would you?" Maria responded with a question, but eyes that said yes.

"I'll get in touch with her tomorrow." Harry was happy to help and to make sure Robert never got close to Maria ever again. No need to discuss details with her, especially not now when the only things she needed were to rest, heal and leave the violent last couple of hours behind her. The years of abuse had come to an end.

"Thanks." Maria felt very tired. Having Harry there next to her felt reassuring as did his taking control over the divorce she already had decided was the right and logical next step to take. This made her comfortable enough to relax and focus on getting better. Once she was released from the hospital she would make the final arrangements and proceed with the divorce.

"I'll leave you to rest now," Harry said as to confirm their understanding.

"Yes I think I need to sleep now."

"I'll be back tomorrow Maria. Just relax and don't worry about anything. I'll call my attorney first thing in the morning."

By the time Harry had reached the door, Maria was already sleeping.

He turned around, smiled at her knowing he would never leave her unprotected again. It was for him an unusual emotion, but one he enjoyed.

On his way out, he ran into Officer Flynn who upon seeing Harry told him he had to question Maria now while her memory was fresh. He looked concerned. Flynn passed him by and with a stoic face entered Maria's room. Harry turned around and followed him.

Harry decided to stay by the door as well. He was concerned by the look on Jim's face.

"Mrs. Cammeresi, I'm sorry to wake you up," he started saying and stopped to take a deep breath. "I'm afraid I have to ask you a couple of questions." He hated this part of the investigation because he really wanted to finish his report, go home, and close the case.

"It's ok, Jim; I know you need some answers. And yes, I must have stabbed Robert with what I now remember was the knife I picked up when he lunged at me. But it was in self-defense."

"Oh, I know, Maria. Your injuries were certainly not self-inflicted."

Harry was holding back, he just stood there listening in on their conversation.

"Could you tell me exactly what happened from the time Robert entered the house?"

"Well, he was actually already in the house when I came back home from work. He had been drinking and was standing in the kitchen having some more of my wine when I told him to leave."

"And what did he do then?"

"He came over to me in a rage, threaten to rape me…after he had hit me first." Maria started to cry and Harry couldn't but come over to her bedside to comfort her. Officer Flynn didn't seem to object having Harry there. It's tough enough to have to ask these questions to a woman who everyone in the village knew as sweet of a person as you could imagine and not allowing her the comfort Harry could provide, Jim thought to himself. Harry took her hand and wiped off the tears from her face, carefully avoiding her left cheek area.

"Take your time Maria," Jim said. "I just want to get the sequence of events right the first time so we don't have to go over this again. So he hit you first, then continued to move towards you, threatened to rape you? Is that correct?"

"Yes." Maria barely whispered the reply.

"And what happened then?"

"When I tried to get away from him, I stumbled and used my hands to hold on to the kitchen counter to avoid falling. I felt something on the table, grabbed it to protect myself not realizing I was holding onto anything sharp, raised my hand to fend him off and must have stabbed him when he launched towards me."

"What happened after that?" Officer Flynn continued.

"He stopped, stared at me, said nothing and left." Maria started shaking again. The shock and the memories, fearing for her life, remembering seeing all the blood made her cry even more. Harry raised his hand as to tell Officer Flynn to stop the interrogation, which he gladly did.

"I believe I have everything I need, Mrs. Cammeresi. May I call you Maria?" She nodded at him with gratitude.

"You rest now and we'll take down a written statement tomorrow." Officer Flynn nodded at Harry, turned around and started walking towards the door. He was just about to leave the room when he turned around again to say:

"I'm sorry; I have one more question, Maria. Do you know where your husband may be?"

"No," she paused. "No idea." Maria answered with a tired and shaky voice.

Harry stayed the night by Maria's side. The following morning he called his lawyer and arranged for her to meet Maria at her earliest convenience. Minutes later Officer Flynn returned. He entered Maria's room with a troubled look on his face.

Chapter Thirteen

"Good Morning, Maria. I hope you had a restful night." Jim looked over at Harry who nodded a yes.

Jim continued after pausing for the longest time. Again he took a deep breath before continuing.

"I'm afraid I have some news that may be upsetting to you," he continued now without hesitation or pause. "Earlier this morning we found a car we believe belonged to your Robert. And in it, we think with high probability, was your husband."

Maria sat up, her mouth falling open, grabbing onto Harry's arm and with an incredulous stare at Officer Flynn's mouth, she waited for him to utter the word dead.

"And I'm sorry to say the person believed to be your husband was found dead inside." Jim carefully checked both Maria and Harry's reactions and found Maria tightening the grip on Harry's arm while Harry stiffened up, his muscles rigid and his facial expression one of disbelief.

"What happened?" he finally, after a long pause and after Maria loosened her grip on his arm, asked with a hesitant and disbelieving voice.

Harry gently helped Maria to lay back down and carefully positioned her head on the pillow. When she, complained about shortness of breath and a racing heartbeat, Harry pushed the button for the nurse who appeared within seconds and asked both Harry and Officer Flynn to leave the room.

"You can come back later if you need to but right now Mrs. Cammeresi needs to rest."

The nurse pushed both Harry and Officer Flynn away towards the door while she, at the same time, assessed the condition of her patient and made the decision to give Maria something to calm her nerves and to get some much needed rest.

"No more visits and questions until I say it's ok." she, in a firm and urging voice told both Officer Flynn and Harry.

Both of them obeyed without protest and left. Once outside Jim replied to Harry's question:

"We obviously don't know what happened but the county police and the crime scene investigators are all over it right now. The car was a total wreck and apparently had caught fire because there wasn't much left of the body inside" Jim replied, covering his mouth as if to avoid throwing up.

"It was a rather gruesome scene and with what was left, a painful death," he continued recalling what he saw upon arriving at the scene at 5am, having only slept four hours. He had spent most of the night yesterday finishing the report he thought would close this case as a domestic dispute turned violent. Next, he had to deal with a body. Or rather what was left of a body whose parts seemed scattered all over inside and outside the vehicle. Jim would forever remember the expression that appeared pained on the burned, and only remaining half of the face still attached to the head of something that once was a human being.

"We were able to identify enough of the license plate number to determine the car belonged to Robert Cammerisi. The crime scene investigators have a forensic odontologist examining the victim's teeth to determine if it is Robert's body we've found."

Harry started to feel a choking sensation in his throat as if he was about to be sick.

"I need some air," he said, turned quickly towards the main entrance, walking quickly outside with Officer Flynn following in his footsteps.

Once they both regained composure, Harry was the first to speak:

"So Jim, was there any other car involved?"

"No, it seems like a single car accident and without any tire marks on the road, the driver was probably speeding, suddenly lost control of the car and skidded off and into the wooded area where the car caught fire with him trapped inside."

Harry felt a quiver in his stomach thinking about the dreadful end Robert had met in that burning car, half of him mutilated before death finally released him from his sorrows and misery.

He started to swallow excessively to shake off the uneasy feeling of nausea.

"We may never know what really happened out there. I'm sure the crime scene investigators will have enough evidence to conclude the cause of death to be accidental due to excessive speed," Jim filled in.

He wanted to close the case without having to bother Maria once more. The knife he found in the kitchen was obviously used to defend her from being struck again. Robert was alive and well enough to drive away. Of course there was a lot of blood in the kitchen but no deadly outcome came of the domestic dispute.

With whatever was left of his body nothing could be concluded other than he had sped off the road, was speared by tree branches and literally sliced in half. He burned into unrecognizable human remains of what once was someone who lived his life as if he was the only one who mattered. Over the last twenty years he had left nothing but a string of misery and pain behind. It seemed only fitting he ended his life in that same way off Route 9N.

Officer Flynn's official report was already on the Chief's desk by morning. Nothing had changed since last night. The car accident had a deadly outcome but Officer Flynn was not in charge of that investigation. It was handled by the county police and its crime scene investigators. It was just another unfortunate speeding accident with a deadly outcome.

Francesca, Maria's oldest daughter, arrived to the hospital when Harry and Jim were going back in to check on Maria's condition. Francesca had gotten a call about her mother a few hours earlier. There seemed to have been some misunderstanding and the hospital had apparently, and in vain, tried to reach Maria's husband Robert on his cell phone. It wasn't until later when they checked with Maria as to how to reach her children.

Upon seeing Officer Flynn, she immediately started asking questions about her mother. Officer Flynn had to, once more, convey the gruesome message to yet another member of the Cammeresi family about Robert's car accident and death.

Francesca stared blankly at Officer Flynn, paused for what felt like an eternity, shrugged half-heartedly before she spoke in a flat voice:

"So that's how he finally got it."

Francesca turned around and with a quick but steady gait disappeared into the hospital to find her mother.

Harry looked at Jim who looked as puzzled as Harry. "He finally got it?" They could only speculate what she meant. Knowing the history and obvious lack of empathy, the comment didn't seem as odd after all.

Chapter Fourteen

Over the next couple of days Cold Spring was far from a sleepy, small town in Putnam County, New York. Wherever you turned, neighbors were talking to each other in a way they normally didn't take the time to do. The topic of their conversation was the same. Maria, the owner of Sweet Maria's Café, had been attacked by her husband Robert, who then fled and killed himself by driving off the road. As if their daughters hadn't had enough grief and sorrow in their lives growing up.

Mrs. Rose was of course in the midst of it all, feeding stories to one and all, without being asked. Surprisingly enough she actually had the good taste of leaving Harry and Maria's past and recent flirtation off the table and sent flowers to her in the hospital. Maybe Maria telling her off the other day had had the intended effect. If so, as surprising as it may be, Maria may have found an ally in Mrs. Rose, who apparently held Maria in high regard.

The support for Maria and her daughters was overwhelming. Returning college kids volunteered to help keep Maria's café in operation while she spent time in Wappinger Falls with her older daughter. The café became a gathering point for the whole village and every time Harry stopped by, he noticed the steady stream of customers lined up, chit-chatting about Maria and the drama that had followed. The village saw the number of coffee drinkers quadruple in just a couple of days. They all wanted to make sure the café she had fought so hard to keep afloat during all those years of struggle, would remain open for a thriving business. It was their way of paying respect to Maria.

Arrangements were made for Robert's funeral by the local mortician. Only the immediate family planned to be there when the ceremony was held the following Thursday. No one in the village was invited. After all, as beloved as Maria was by the villagers, was how hated her now dead husband was by the community.

There were still of course practical matters to deal with and thankfully Maria had the whole village of Cold Spring and her two daughters helping her through it all. Thanks to all the help and love she received, she could take her time to get over the very traumatic end of her marriage and accidental death of Robert. The thought that somehow, the injuries she had inflicted when he lunged himself at her had something to do with the crash. These thoughts, made for an uneasy period of time. But when Officer Flynn had called to tell her that the county police had ruled speeding was the cause of the accident, she felt she could finally let go and leave it behind her.

This was the version Officer Flynn told Maria. The official version was more like what Jim had seen with his own eyes. He thought it was of no use telling Maria about the more likely, slow and excruciating death of Robert.

Harry had left Maria alone to grieve with her family. He had checked in on her right before she was released and picked up by Francesca, and they had agreed to wait until after the funeral to see each other. Harry had

105

called his attorney to tell her that there was no further need for a divorce lawyer but to instead speak to Maria about helping her with the financial ramifications of Robert's passing. With no will at hand, it was an easy transition of assets. Maria had decided to set up her own will in case anything would happen to her; something his attorney was happy to arrange.

To keep his mind off the dramatic last couple of days, he had turned to what he always did when he had to deal with things he felt uncomfortable with and didn't know how to handle. He buried himself in research and right now the most exciting task ahead was to identify the people in the photograph. He hadn't spoken to Joe but planned to do so soon. What day is it today he thought to himself? He was sitting in his favorite reading chair with a glass of Merlot - yes, he had discovered the wonderful aroma of red wine by chance when he had visited the wine and liquor store the day of Maria's dismissal from the hospital. Mike, the wine connoisseur, had challenged him to try something else than his usual Chardonnay and recommended a Merlot from 14 Hands Vineyards, a place where they celebrate the spirit of the wild horses that once roamed the Columbia River Basin in the state of Washington. The tough little horses were only 14 hands in height. The wine is a round, structured Merlot, packed with rich flavor and aroma of blackberry, plum, cherry and mocha - a balanced Merlot. Or that's how Mike explained the wine, and the reason why Harry should give it a try.

It turned out to be delicious and Harry couldn't help himself thinking about his friend Joe who, like the smaller horses didn't reach far enough up to be the ones mostly desired or appreciated but who still thrived because of their wild instincts and toughness.

Harry reached for his Iphone to check the day. Today was Thursday. The day of the funeral. Maybe Maria will be back at her house Saturday. I don't really want to bother her he thought but I can't wait to talk to her about the photograph. The familiarity with the photo and believing she had seen it before was really exciting news. He paused to examine the picture in front of him. His eyebrows furrowed and then released as if to add confusion to what he was actually seeing. A picture of a family, apparently from Italy since the Italian word for arrived ("arrivati") was scribbled on the back of the photo, dated July 17, 1945. Harry leaned forward, sliding his chair closer to the photograph to take it all in. Where were they from? Umbria - the home of Maria's family? Are some of them still alive? Where do they live now? Did they, like many of the Italian immigrants at the time, end up in New York?

Harry had many questions and few answers but exuded calm and focus knowing that this challenge was right up his alley and with help from Maria they would solve this mystery. He ran through what he must do, leaned forward again, hands clutched together, eager to get going with determination to find them.

Maybe I could suggest a quiet dinner with Maria at my place on Saturday, Harry speculated. She may appreciate not having to think about anything—especially a cooked meal. Enjoying dinner, a relaxing evening in good company after a turbulent week, he thought to himself while taking another sip of the wonderful Merlot that Mike had recommended. I better listen to his wine advice from now on. Harry smiled thinking how adventurous he was with everything else but how conservative he was with his wine choices. Oh, well, it's all about not knowing enough and taking the easy way out rather than being spontaneous enough to try something new. He was happy he had listened to Mike and made the decision to step outside his "wine comfort zone."

He was just about to put the photograph away when the phone rang.

"This is Harry, who is this?" he said in quick succession.

"My name is Frank. I'm a friend of Joe. I think you know that sorry piece of shit.."

Harry shifted position on the chair, unable to get comfortable, while Frank continued:

"You have a photograph I'm very interested in knowing more about and I believe you are the man I need to meet. Joe mentioned you were on it. So, have you found out who the fucking bastards are?"

Chapter Fifteen

Harry felt a flush of adrenaline course through his body. Annoyed more than angry he carefully controlled his voice and tone while answering Frank's questions:

"Not sure what you are talking about. Was it Frank you said your name was?"

"Yeah, I'm Frank. So what do you have for me?" he asked with an irritated and impatient, raised voice.

The tightness in Harry's jaw and facial muscles and the squinting of his eyes were obvious signs of how irritated he felt about this conversation. What fucking right did Joe have to give my phone number to Frank?

Harry poked his tongue lightly into his cheek to help relax and took a long breath before answering with a raised voice:

"Hey Frank, I think you should talk to Joe and not me. I may be helping Joe but if you need information do not call ME. Call your friend Joe and he can tell you what you need to know. Is that understood?"

Harry who normally didn't snap at people was pissed, feeling heat flush through his body, pulse speeding and heartbeat pounding. He couldn't believe how he was telling off Frank who he of course knew was part of the mob and a dangerous man.

Frank, surprised by having Harry speak to him in such a candid way shut down, not responding for what

Harry thought was an eternity. He believed that Frank had disconnected. Then he finally replied:

"I'm not sure you know what you are talking about and you definitely don't seem to know WHO you are talking to. But never mind, I'll fucking call the sorry piece of shit myself. You just do your job finding out where I can locate the people in the photo."

Frank slammed down his phone on the desk in front of him but Harry could hear him saying "Shit, this isn't going fast enough." before the call was disconnected. Harry, leaning back in his chair took a deep breath of relief and emptied his glass of Merlot. In one sweeping and quick move he stood up, rushed outside and headed up Main Street to Joe's store.

Chapter Sixteen

"What are you doing?" Harry slammed the door behind him and gave Joe a flinty stare, his eyes tight and his face red and sweaty after running all the way up Main Street to Joe's store.

"What were you thinking, giving out my number to Frank?" A vein on Harry's throat twitched with every sweeping arm gesture. This was the second time in a very short period that Harry had lost his cool and calm. With an irritated tone he snapped at Joe, and without listening to Joe's half-hearted excuse, he added:

"Especially to a mobster who you know as well as I do is a dangerous killer. Why take these risks now after all these years? Why is he so damn interested in finding the family in the photo?"

Joe, hands up, palm towards Harry as if to defend himself from his friend's anger, was just about to say something when Harry slowly shaking his head and with a heavy sigh and much more controlled voice said:

"Alright Joe, the damage is done. It can't be undone. Let's just make sure we keep my personal life out of this, shall we? If you get me any more involved with this psychopath, you'll find out that I'm a worse offender than he is."

Joe, visibly sweating, ears turning red and with a trembling chin finally answered in a stammering voice:

"Yes, yes, I know I..I shouldn't have. It won't happen again Harry. I swear."

Joe didn't like it when he was treated this way, especially not by Harry. It actually annoyed him that he of all people didn't treat him with respect. What did he know about Frank and a life to which he had never been exposed, never had to fear. Harry had lived a protected and luxurious life compared to Joe's existence, having to fight for everything and do anything necessary to survive, And now when he needed Harry to help him with a favor to keep Frank off his back, he got pissed about something as simple as having given out his phone number.

"I'll take care of it," he said with a displeased and irritated voice. Crossing his arms to look more determined and tougher than he was, he still looked like a minor league player next to Harry who by lifting his hand loosely, palm up in a "who cares" gesture, dismissed Joe's offer by simply saying:

"You asked me to help you and that's what I'm going to do. But it's going to be on my terms. So please, no more decisions without conferring with me first."

Joe, with his head bowed, backed up against the wall behind the counter, felt once more degraded, worthless and cheap. And he hated the feeling. They'll see. I've done a lot more in my life than Frank and Harry ever had to do. I'm not afraid of anyone or anything and no one should be treating me like I don't know what to do. The frustration at how he was being treated made his blood pump faster and he was already deep in thoughts as how to best seek revenge and show them who was the toughest of the three men.

"So, Joe," Harry interrupted Joe's petty thoughts, "what are you going to do about getting Frank off my back?"

"I'll deal with Frank," Joe said in a low voice, rubbing the back of his neck and avoiding eye contact with Harry. He was nervous and didn't like having the ball back in his court after having successfully passed it to Harry that morning over a week ago.

"Good Joe. I'll continue my research and I'll let you know what I find and what my next move is, as long as you make sure I don't have to speak to or see Frank ever again."

Harry was satisfied for now but far from relieved with Joe's reply. He knew all too well having been a guard at the correction facility back in California, that once convicts had served time, they said and promised what they needed to say. Joe wasn't any different from other ex-cons. Harry knew it, yet he had developed an unusual friendship with Joe but couldn't trust him.

"Maria had mentioned to me that she actually recognized the photograph when I showed it to her about a week ago. It really surprised me, but it may be a very important piece of the puzzle." Harry continued as if what he just had thought about not trusting Joe hadn't sunk in.

Joe, lifting his eyebrows surprised and with a floating sensation, like all his burdens had been removed, smiled at the very good news.

"Maria's mother emigrated from Italy in the 50s right?" Joe eagerly asked.

"I believe so," Harry responded and continued "I think I'll see her over the weekend and I'll ask more about her mother. But like I said Joe, this information stays between you and me. I'll find the family as a favor to you, not Frank."

Joe knew. He knew exactly what made Harry spring into action. He saw the glimmer of being challenged in his eyes and knew he'd take it without hesitating or thinking about the consequences. Joe appeared relaxed again, content and convinced Harry would find the people in the photo for him and once Harry did, he'd be there to finish it, he thought to himself. He started to hum "O Sole Mio" when Harry turned around to leave. "Che bella cosa è na jurnata 'e sole, n'aria serena dopo na tempesta." (What a beautiful thing is a sunny day, the air is serene after a storm.)

Harry would later regret having revealed the connection between Maria and the family in the picture.

Chapter Seventeen

The day of the funeral passed. He had called Maria in the morning before the 11:00am funeral service to see how she was doing. It became clear to him that she was more relieved than sad about putting her abusive, non-supportive husband and father of the children to rest.

Maria and her daughters had, after some rough teenage years, found peace and an undivided love and appreciation for each other. No tears or emotions were displayed and the short service was over in little more than 15 minutes. No words about this man who no one missed were spoken. The funeral was simply a necessity, not a tribute.

During their conversation in the morning, Maria suggested they should get together for dinner on Saturday evening. Harry was relieved he didn't have to ask and invited her for dinner at his place. He felt akward asking her over so soon after the funeral, but Robert hadn't been part of Maria's life for long periods of time, only to reappear in one last miserable event.

Harry had spent most of the week since the night of the attack on Maria and the whole day researching emigration from Italy to the U.S. during World War II and after the war ended. He wanted to find out why, at the time, when the photograph was taken, Italians made the decisions to leave for what could only be assumed a search for a better life in the U.S. The date July 17, 1945 with the italian word "arrivati" (arrived) written next to it indicating the family had arrived...but where? New York? Harry knew very little about life in Italy during and right after World War II but realized that finding out more would be essential in aiding him in his search for the family.

After visits to local libraries and extensive online searches, Harry had found that over the next decade following the war 600,000 Italians arrived to the United States. But why would a family move from Perugia in Umbria? That is if the family was from the same area as Maria's mother. Harry made the assumption that they were, considering Maria whose mother was from that region, recognized the photo. It was like looking for a needle in a haystack. How many could possibly have arrived to United States from Umbria, Italy on that specific day of July 17, 1945?

If he could narrow down his search to the region of Umbria, and even down to the town of Perugia, he could maybe find what he was looking for.. He felt tempted to call Maria but wisely decided to wait. One thing was clear to him. Most Italians who emmigrated to the United States up until the the beginning of the war were Sicilians and poor farmers who weren't well treated by the more educated and wealthier industrialized northerners.

It wasn't until after the war ended, he discovered that the professionally trained Italians arrived in the states. During the war, Umbria was heavily bombed and in the summer of 1944 became a battlefield between the allied forces and the retreating Germans. Was that the reason for them moving, maybe fleeing from the war zone? Harry thought while pouring another glass of the Merlot from the 14 Hands Vineyard. Sipping on it he leaned forward while sitting in his favorite chair by the window facing the sun that was just about to set over the mountains on the other side of the Hudson River. Something in the picture he had investigated caught his eye.

Behind the family and in the distance you could see a sign on a building. The picture was taken outside and by the look of it, close to a factory of some kind. Harry rose quickly from his chair, almost knocking his glass of wine off the armrest. He went to his work desk, opened up the drawer and returned back to his wine and chair with a magnifier in his hand. The sign was blurry and far away from where the family was standing. He moved the magnifier around to get the best possible angle. Then Harry put the magnifier glass down. Despite the distance he was sure that what he saw was the clue he had been waiting for.

What was clearly visible was a sign that read PERUGINA.

Chapter Eighteen

The family picture was definately taken in Perugia, Umbria. Perugina was the maker of the famous Bacio chocolate. The factory was located in Perugia, and had been there ever since the early 1900s when the company was founded. Maria had a sweet tooth and Bacio was one of her favorite chocolates growing up, usually invitingly putting one between her lips for Harry to "kiss away." The Bacio usually led from one thing to another and soon the chocolates became a fun part of the sex they explored as young adults. To this day, Maria was selling the famous Perugina chocolate and the chocolate covered hazelnut, wrapped in a love note, at her cafe'.

Harry took a sip from his third glass of Merlot and leaned back, his mind wandering off to several nights before when Maria had stayed over and the chair had turned into a sled launch for a playful, sensual and intense deep and fiery penetration, her body rocking on top of him. He closed his eyes and felt his manhood grow, wanting her and her lips, moving his hand down to touch himself, his mind focused on Maria's sexy and inviting body. Her soft skin; her breasts perfectly fitting in the palm of his hands; nipples that hardened under his careful touch when she methodically and teasingly moved closer.

The phone rang.

Harry catapulted in a hurry off the chair like a rocket. The wine glas moved like a pendelum back and forth, as if to illustrate the erotic swings Harry experienced as he awoke from his day dream. The glass found its footing on the sidetable. Still half-delirous with pleasant thoughts, he picked up the phone.

"This is Harry," he said taking deep breaths in succession.

"Hi Harry." The soft voice on the other end was a welcome surprise.

"Oh, hi Maria," Harry blushed without realizing it.

"You sound out of breath Harry. Did I catch you at a bad moment?" she said apologetically with a tired voice.

"Oh, not at all. I was just sipping on a glass of wine," he replied leaving his day dreaming to himself. "I'm sorry but I didn't want to bother you earlier. How was the service?"

"You know, Harry. It was proper but I would lie if I said it was anything else."

Maria made her feelings about the funeral well known to Harry a couple of days before, knowing that what she expected to feel was more relief than sorrow, especially after his final act of humilation, anger and violent behavior.

"Do you mind if I come over?"

Harry, who still had the image of a naked Maria fresh on his mind, wasn't sure how to respond, thinking he may have inappropriately thought about her in a sexual way the day of her, abusive and not missed, husband's funeral.

Maria continued without waiting for his reply:

"I came back earlier than expected. The kids and I had lunch together and I thought it was better for me to get back home. Fransesca wanted me to stay one more night with her but to be honest with you Harry - I really felt a wave of relief and just wanted to slip into something comfortable with a glass of wine by myself."

Harry, still with the image of a naked Maria fresh in mind, didn't get a chance to reply before she added:

"But once I got back home, the house felt so cold and threating...I don't think I can spend the night here..."

Harry interupted her.

"Of course Maria. Of course you can come over. Are you hungry?"

"Not really Harry. Did you eat something?"

"Not yet. Just come over and I'll put something together for us."

"Thanks Harry. I'll be over in half an hour. Just want to put a few things together."

Harry wasn't sure what to think. He was happy that she had called him on the eve of the funeral, but confused about how he felt about it. He had never been the type who was there for a woman in need of comfort, as much as he was used to getting satisfied by them. He shrugged off the feeling, a feeling of guilt and shame thinking of Maria in those primal terms. She was different. He knew that and she meant a lot more to him than any other woman had before.

"I'll bring a bottle of red," Maria said and interupted the silence that had followed.

"Not necessary, Maria. I picked up a dozen of my new favorite Merlot the other day and have plenty of wine."

"Ok Harry, I'll see you soon then," she said with nervous anticipation,

About half an hour later Maria was comfortably sitting with a glass of red on the sofa, her legs up and folded to her side and with a blanket wrapped around her.

"Sorry, I don't know why I was so chilly, but the wine, the blanket and you making...well what are you making out there in the kitchen?" she in a curious voice asked Harry from across the room.

"Just putting together a chicken salad. And I think you need to try it. It's really good if I may say so myself." Harry, the bachelor, preferred to prepare his own meals when not traveling. The hotel and restaurant food had gotten to him after all these years and he enjoyed cooking and exploring new receipes when back in Cold Spring. But a dinner for two was always a more exciting proposition, especially if the guest turned out to be Maria.

"Ok, I trust you and your cooking. Of course I'll have some. The wine is stimulating my taste buds," Maria replied thinking that the wine stimulated more than just that...

Her heart skipped a beat in excitement and anticipation of what lay in front of her. Not just tonight but the prospect of many more nights with Harry. She did have mixed feelings of shame and guilt going from her husband's funeral to her lover's bed on the same evening. She quickly shrugged them off, allowing her true feelings to decide what was right and wrong. And there was no wrong in being liberated and feeling happiness and love after years of suffering.

After a light dinner, a bottle of wine and passionate kisses on the warm and cozy sofa, they moved to the bedroom. The air full of sweet romantic and promising summer sounds from the opened window accompanied their rythmic intertwined naked bodies to eagerly satisfy each others lustful desires.

Tomorrow was going to reveal a very important clue to the identity of the family in the photo, that for now remained peacefully on top of the research pile, next to Harry's favorite reading chair. But tonight the bed, not the reading chair, was the focus of their full attention, and with a lot more significance and importance than they could ever have imagined those hot summer days years ago.

They fell asleep, lulled by the soothing music of the Hudson Rivers ebb and flow outside the open bedroom window, unaware of the risks and dangers lurking around the corner and how the picture would end up changing their lives.

They never saw it coming.

Chapter Nineteen

Harry awoke first.

The white tulle curtain fluttered in the wind that through the open window filled the bedroom with its warm summer like air. It was only the month of April and the calendar still said spring but summer had arrived early and Harry enjoyed every minute of it. He turned his head ever so slightly to his left and got a first look at Maria on this beatiful morning. The thin sheet wrapped around her legs like a twister, leaving her right breast and shoulder exposed. Her face had an expression of satisfaction. A relaxed, peaceful and beautiful smile as if she was having a dream from which she didn't want to wake up .

Harry carefully, not to disturb her, got up and walked naked into the kitchen, measured up five spoons of his favorite Lavazza Crema e Gusto coffee, poured four cups of water in the machine and heated up three crescente in the microwave, while taking out the imported Italian peach preserves. Soon the kitchen smelled like the B&B in Tuscany he had visited on one of his trips - beautiful La Foce outside Pienza.

Maria woke up to the smell of childhood. The soft warm air and the beams of sunshine spread joy and happiness. The aroma of freshly made coffee and baked crescente - in her Mom's case a double espresso to start the day, brought back memories. Her Mom, Cristina, usually brought the espresso and crescente to Maria's room to wake her up. She, when time allowed for it, snuggled up next to her and positioned the cup right under Maria's nose to let her enjoy the aroma of a well balanced, full-bodied, round and smooth espresso. Sometimes her Mom allowed her a taste. At her young age it proved to be a very bitter drink. A taste she would later describe as "a brewed hot drink that coats your tongue like condensed milk." But, back then, Maria when allowed to take a sip felt like a grown up. The morning routine was the best time of the day for Maria, right before her Mom rushed over to the cafe' and the young girl walked the short distance to her elementary school.

"Good morning, my Pearl." Harry leaned over and put a cup of espresso right under her nose.

Maria laughed.

"I know you told me you wanted to go back to work at the cafe today so I took the liberty of making you a quick early breakfast," Harry continued to talk when Maria realized that the man right in front of her with a cup of espresso in one hand and a crescente in the other, was completely naked from top to toe. She couldn't keep herself from staring. For him walking around naked was second nature--at least when at home. Maria smiled when thinking of Harry walking up Main Street naked in nothing but what the creator had adorned him.

Maria couldn't stop wondering what she may miss in her very subjective assessment of him. I mean, she thought to herself, this is a man who seems to have everything, physically that is. He gives an impression of being financially sound and without a doubt having an appetite for life and adventure.

Harry turned around to go back into the kitchen and Maria laughed again at the sight of him casually attending to the kitchen chores while she quickly finished her espresso, went into the bathroom to shower and get ready for her first day back at her beloved cafe.

What a nice new fresh start of her life she was thinking when Harry joined her in the shower. The cafe she thought would open late that morning.

Francesca had already arrived not knowing if her mom was going to start work today or not. She also wondered, when stopping by the house earlier, why there was no sight of her Mom having spent the night there. It wasn't like she was concerned. Both her daughters knew the history between Harry and their Mom and anyone who knew them both would have to be blind not to see the affection they obviously had for each other, even after all these years.

"Hi Mom," Francesca greeted her mom with a hug, a kiss on her left cheek, avoiding the still tender right side.

"Sorry Francesca, I forgot to tell you I was going to go back to work today. You drove all the way down here." Maria apologetically and frantically gestured with her arms in the air.

"Don't worry Mom. And by the way good thing I did since you are late." Francesca turned to Maria and winked her eye.

"Well, maybe I do have some explaining to do..." Maria started off saying in a reverse role play having to explain to her daughter where she spent the night and with whom.

" Chill," Franscesa interupted her with a casual, new generation, way of looking at life reply. It was more of an "oh well, rather than a what if" approach leading to an understanding that if nothing bad happens then you are ok. To be asking yourself "what if" never really solves anthing but a math equation. What does matter is "oh well, you had an experience and experiences enrich your life." Francesca and her sister had gone through the school of life with a drug and alcohol addicted father and having to deal with their own addictions to drugs in their early teens. The "what if" meant absolutely nothing to them.

Maria said no more and in silence went about making sure everything was in order and ready to serve her first customer. Francesca left but not before she leaned over and with a smile that warmed Maria's heart whispered in her Mom's ear "I love the after shave Harry is using." Maria blushed, gave Franscesa a hug and kiss, feeling blessed to have such a wonderful and understanding daughter.

To her surprise, it wasn't Mrs Rose who entered at the same time Francesca was leaving, but Joe, who only once in a blue moon showed up at her cafe.

"Good morning, Maria. I'm sorry for your loss. I heard that the funeral was yesterday. How are you coping?" Joe didn't really care. He was not there to see if Maria needed any help or support. He was there because he couldn't get the photograph off his mind. Frank had called again last night to complain that things didn't move along fast enough. Joe knew he needed to get the ball rolling. Frank wasn't going to sit and wait for him or Harry to figure things out. He needed answers, and he needed them yesterday.

"Good morning, Joe and thanks for your concern. I'm doing fine. You know, like the rest of the village, the circumstances and, for a very long time, strained relationship I had with Robert. Nothing can come as a big surprise to you when I say I'm fine." Maria thougth it was better to just come out right away saying what everyone already knew to be the truth.

"Oh, I didn't mean to poke into your private life, Maria," Joe started off saying when she interupted him:

"You didn't, Joe. My private life is my private life to the extent it is possible to keep anything private in this small village. What can I do for you this morning? It 's not every morning I see you here and especially not as my first customer." Maria smiled but it couldn't keep her from wondering and worrying what brought him to her cafe at this early hour.

"Oh, nothing special," Joe lied. "But I would like to get an ice coffee this morning. In this summer like weather a cool drink is what we need to get things done wouldn't you say Maria?"

"Small, medium or large?" Maria asked still confused, wondering what he meant by getting things done...

"I'll have a medium please," Joe replied, took a seat at the nearest table with an unobstracted view of the street and entrance. He didn't want to be interrupted by anyone walking in unnoticed, and especially not Harry.

"I was wondering," Joe started saying while Maria poured the coffee in a medium cup and leaned down to the freezer unit to pick up some ice. "Where was your mother born?"

"Perugia, in Italy," Maria replied and added "why do you ask Joe?"

"Oh, just wondering now after all you've gone through lately that you may be interested in knowing more about the past."

Maria thought the whole conversation and Joe's reason for asking about his mother was weird. On the other hand, Joe wasn't known as the most intelligent, nor socially skilled person in town. His customers were few and the ones visiting his store seemed to be tourists and townies who had gotten to know Joe and his quirky behavior and peculiar social skills. Well, calling it skills might be an overstatement.

"I'm not sure there's that much more to know about my past since my mother didn't tell me a lot about her days in Italy and how she met her American war hero, got pregnant with me, then left to fend for herself when he decided to move on to another woman. She did what she had to do to survive. If you are looking for a hero look no further. She is the one." Maria handed over the ice coffee to Joe, who took another quick glance out the window before continuing:

"Did she maybe leave anything behind about her past in Italy? I mean, you know, some memories she wanted to keep, like photos, letters and such?"

Maria, now used to Joe's inquisitive questioning, stopped thinking about the strange reasons Joe may have for asking. Instead she let her mind wander back in time just like she had this morning when waking up in Harry's bed thinking she was that nine-year old girl, smelling her mom's espresso under her nose.

"You know what Joe, I do remember growing up that she showed me some pictures and letters she had from her time in Italy. Now when you mention it I think I'll look for those this weekend. Probably somewhere in the attic that I need to go through anyway now when I'm moving"?

"Moving?" Joe raised his eyebrows and looked up from his ice coffee and with a surprise look on his face continued: "Are you moving?"

Maria didn't know why she said she she was moving.

"Nothing decided of course, just a thought I have that I've outlived the old house and especially after what happened. It's also is in dire need of repair and I may be better off selling," Maria quickly added.

Joe grabbed his ice coffee, said a quick goodbye to Maria and started walking towards the door when he turned around and added:

"You know Maria, let me know what you find, will you? I have boxes of old postcards and letters in my store. If you like to sell anything from your house, now that you may be moving and all, let me know. I'll be happy to get you some good prices for what you have that you no longer want to keep, ok?"

Maria nodded while Joe, in a rush, left. He smiled, surprised and content with all the information he had been able to find out this morning, when exciting the cafe.

He started to whistle "O sole mio..."

Chapter Twenty

Maria locked the door behind her. It had been a busy day but felt good to be back on her normal schedule. All her regulars had stopped by to welcome her back, including Mrs. Rose who of course was more interested in knowing if she enjoyed the flower arrangement she received from her in the hospital and what Maria planned to do now that her husband had passed and left her alone in the empty house.

For someone who was supposed to know everything and everybody's private life in town, she seemed to have lost some of her instincts of late, or was it just a trick to get Maria to open up about her plans. Maria wasn't sure. After all Mrs. Rose was in her early 80s and by now dementia may have started to affect her staying on top of things, Maria thought while strolling up Main Street and turning left onto her street.

She hesitated, stopped for a second and was thinking that maybe she should turn around and go back down to Harry. She shrugged off the uneasy feeling. I need to do this, getting used to living in my own house despite the incident and recent bad memories, she thought to herself when stepping onto the porch, unlocking the door and entering the hallway. Continuing towards and entering the kitchen where she had been beaten up only a couple of weeks before, she started to shake.

She reached out for a glass, opened up a bottle of wine, and sat down on the floor right next to where she had been attacked. Her eyes dull, lifeless and her bottom lip trembling. She quickly took two big sips of her wine. Uncontrolled tears flowed down her cheeks. She drew her knees up to her chin, locked tight together and covered her face with both hands. The embarrassment was worse than the incident itself. How could she have allowed it to happen? Her mind was struggling with her desire to run away from the experience of the past week and the inability of not having taken the opportunity to escape a long time ago, away from the years of pain and humiliation. It was terrible.

After a long period of contemplation, her disapointment turned slowly into relief now that everything was finally over. Her relief turned into elation, eyes now wide and glowing and tears of anger turned into happy tears. Her cheeks shining and her heartbeat raced as she thought about what a wonderful future she now had to consider. With another two big sips of wine she rose from the floor triumphant and confident that she had found happiness.

Chapter Twenty One

Harry had spent another day on the internet, using the online resources of Ellis Island and others, collecting information about the immigrants from Italy to United States during and after World War II. It was, as always, fascinating for him to learn new things and to become completly engulfed in another adventure.

He now knew he needed to plan for a trip to Italy and the town of Perugia to try to find more clues as to the fate of this family who seemed to draw a lot of his attention.

Harry knew that what he may find out wasn't necessarily going to shed light over why Frank was so interested in finding them but he was determined to find the truth, whatever the consequences were. He had never had any fear about what may be hiding under a rock when turned over. Harry was a journalist in that respect. Whatever it takes to find something, and whatever or whoever may be in the way of the process doesn't matter as long as by turning the rock over the truth is revealed.

I'll take my chances he thought, and assume they arrived on July 17, 1945 to New York City and not any other port in the U.S. How many people could possibly have arrived on that specific day from Italy, and especially from Perugia? This will definately narrrov it down to a handful of families, if not even less.

Harry felt a tremendous satisfaction having, in part by chance and in part due to his diligent research, found enough already to start planning his departure to Perugia, Italy.

And then of course, it was that rather peculiar fact that Maria had recognized the photo. He was hoping that would lead to even more revealing information about the family's background.

He paused and looked up from the pile of handwritten notes and information. Eyes wide open in excitement, adrenaline rushing through his body when thinking about how great it would be to travel to Italy, not alone as he normally did when traveling, but to take Maria with him. She could look for her ancestors while I did my investigation into the family in the picture. What a great way of spending time with her and for her to get away for a while, especially after everything that had recently transpired.

He decided to ask her tomorrow at brunch hoping she would say yes. They had decided to meet up at noon at The Hudson Hil's Café and Market on Main Street after they kissed each other goodbye earlier in the morning, right before Maria in a rush left to open up her café.

Chapter Twenty Two

Maria spent a good half an hour in the shower.

It was a relief to rinse off the past, focusing on the future and enjoy the moment. She stroked her arm, mirroring the movement of Harrys' hand touching her ever so gently, her skin covered in a fresh soapy feeling as soft as when he first touched her back in high school. Her muscles relaxed, losing the tension she felt when entering the house earlier and that now felt less like a home and more like a prison she was ready to escape from.

The water streamed down her face and her tongue darted out to catch some of it, touching her lips. In her mind she felt Harry's lips touching hers, their tongues meeting in a passionate dance; a conversation between their bodies and souls. Her body craved Harry, a feeling of lightheadedness and a shiver that brought pleasure and a quickening breath and breathlessness. She lifted her chin to expose her neck, thrust out her breasts, allowing the water to stream down her naked body, slightly parted her legs, her fingers gently touching herself like she so very much desired and, after all these years of being denied, with a satisfaction she thought was long passed her age.

Getting out of the shower took some convincing but the soft robe, a glass of wine and her favorite love sofa convinced her.

Maria put her legs up, curled to her side - her favorite position, took a sip of the wine and thought to herself that the last couple of weeks had been the most dramatic weeks of her life, but also the most exhilarating. How can a person, in the span of two weeks, be beaten and almost raped by her husband, who the same evening, ended up dead on the side of the road, and yet find love that had been lost for so many years?

Her thoughts wandered off to the past, tears of joy trickling down her cheeks when thinking of her mother who did so much to give her a chance to succeed as the first generation American.

What was it Joe had said earlier in the day? After all she had been going through maybe she should start finding out more about her Italian heritage and past. He does have a point, Maria thought to herself when she, with vigor, rose up from her comfortable position on the sofa.

She hardly ever visited the attic after the kids stopped using it as their hiding place. She didn't know what to expect, or how she would react to finding parts and pieces of a past she had mixed feelings about.

Maria spent a good couple of hours going through not only her kids' toys but her own from way back. It brought back memories, smiles and tears of joy. Joe was right. It was actually important for her to find out more about her heritage and past now when a new beginning of her life was waiting to happen.

Right before she was about to go back downstairs she laid eyes on an old box all the way in the back left corner of the attic. She immediately knew. This was the box her mom had showed her right before she passed away.

She, with trembling hands, opened up the box not knowing what to expect. To her surprise and shock, her heartbeat racing, the first thing she saw was a picture she recognized.

She also found some letters to her mother from a Mrs. Rachel Perugino dated back to the early 1940's.

On the back of the photograph, the following message was handwritten in Italian "Grazie per il vostro aiuto con Angelina e Eduardo - Signora Perugino" [Thank you for all your help with Angelina and Eduardo - Mrs Perugino].

The photo was an exact copy of the same photo Harry had showed her that evening at the Half Moon Bay restaurant in Dobbs Ferry.

Chapter Twenty Three

They met as planned at The Hudson Hil's Café and Market the following day at noon.

"Good morning, Maria," Harry greeted her, rising from his seat, giving her a gentle kiss on her cheek while pulling out her chair. He had picked one of the small café tables on the porch. This way they could speak without being overheard he thought.

"Did you have a relaxing evening, Maria?" Harry asked at the same time the waitress came over with the menus.

"Yes and a very interesting one," she answered. "I went through some old boxes in the attic and found one that my mother had brought with her from Italy. She showed it to me right before she passed, but I had totally forgotten about it."

"Tell me, what was in the box?" Harry eagerly and impatiently asked while taking a quick look at the menu, deciding in a blink that he wanted the gravlax and eggs brunch.

"Do you remember I told you I recognized the photo you showed me at the Half Moon restaurant?

"Yeah…

"Well, I found the photo in the box my mother had brought over from Italy when she moved here after the war."

"That's fantastic." Harry couldn't have been happier. Everything seemed to fit like a hand in a glove. "Did you find any messages, names or reasons for her bringing it over all the way from Italy?" Harry asked, too excited to place his brunch order when the waitress returned. "Give us a few more minutes, will you please?"

The waitress turned around, almost annoyed by Harry's indecision and dismissal of her.

"I did." Maria looked straight into Harry's green eyes wondering if he would ask her to join him, knowing that he would leave for Italy as soon as she told him the rest of what she had found in the box. This time she wanted to get away from everything here in Cold Spring and join him on one of his adventures she, up until know only had heard about. She was ready to experience one herself. What could be more perfect than to join him in Perugia Italy, the country and place her mother had left for a better life here in the States. She had many times thought about tracing her own heritage, but her life had always made it impossible, until now, when strange circumstances had made it possible.

"There were letters from a Mrs. Perugino to my mother and a handwritten message on back of the picture," Maria continued and handed over the picture to Harry. He took a quick glance at it and the writing on the back. It was definitely the same picture Joe had received from Frank.

"What does the message mean?" Harry asked since his Italian was limited to ordering food at a restaurant.

"It means thank you for all your help with Angelina and Eduardo, and signed by Mrs. Perugino."

"The letters," Maria continued, "Mrs. Perugino wrote my mother were all about her two children Angelina and Eduardo and how they couldn't stop talking about my mother and all the fun they always had with her. She apparently baby sat Angelina and from time to time her younger brother Eduardo as well.

"That's amazing," Harry yelled, the other guests turning around, curious about what was going on. He lowered his voice and continued: "Your mother baby sat the very same family I am going to try and find." Harry still too busy to order his brunch turned away the waitress once more and who now didn't hide her frustration, turning to Maria and asked:

"Would you like to order something maybe...?"

Maria placed an order for two gravlax and eggs, two mimosas and two glass of tap water, knowing that gravlax was Harry's favorite brunch food.

"You know, Maria," Harry continued without paying any attention to the waitress or Maria's order, "this is the best news I have had in a long time and now we need to plan our trip to Italy."

Did Maria just hear him say, "our trip to Italy?" She leaned over the table, kissed Harry and couldn't care less about the curious looks from the villagers sitting next to them on the porch.

"What did I do to deserve that?" Harry clueless, not realizing what he had just said, continued not expecting an answer, "Do you think you could have your daughters take care of your café again for a couple of weeks?"

*

Plans were set in motion that same afternoon. Maria spoke to Francesca and Serafina who gladly said yes to taking care of the café while their mom finally got a chance to spend time with the man she loved. And they were excited about finding out more about their grandmother's past. Harry, now definitely knowing the family was from Perugia, also had a name. He booked the flight for two to Rome, leaving in seven days. Maria had to arrange for an express passport that promised to be ready within forty eight hours.

He knew he would be able trace down the family roots in Perugia and maybe even locate some of the family relatives left behind when they moved to the U.S. The answers were to be found there, not here. The only way was to go back in time and find their ancestors in Perugia. What better way of doing so than in the company of Maria and her desire to trace her roots.

Harry had never been happier but things had almost gone too easy, too smooth and too fast for his liking. He wasn't complaining though. Most of his trips and research in the past had taken a lot more time and effort but with Maria joining him he felt this could be a perfect combination of work and pleasure. He hadn't looked forward to a trip this much in a long, long time.

Two days after their brunch, late in the evening, someone was knocking on Maria's door. She was in the kitchen having a late dinner and didn't think it was strange that someone would, unannounced, stop by her house. As a matter of fact she was convinced it was Harry stopping by so to her surprise, when opening the door ready to greet Harry with a kiss, she instead was looking at the much less attractive Joe.

Chapter Twenty Four

"Joe…I was expecting to see someone else." Maria said.

"I bet, Maria. Harry wasn't available so he sent me."

"Sent you?"

"Not exactly, I'm just kidding. I wanted to stop by to hear what you may have found in your attic. Anything you want to sell now that you are moving?"

"Not sure I understand?"

"Well, you know when I visited you at the café and we talked about it being time for you to move and you were going to look for some old pictures and letters from Italy. Did you find out more about your past? You know I'm always interested in old things to sell in my store so if you have anything you'd like to get rid of I'll be glad to help out in any way I can."

Frank had contacted Joe earlier that same day and he wasn't happy with Joe's progress, or lack thereof. Things were not happening fast enough and he was furious at Joe for not getting anywhere. He demanded result within 48 hours.

Maria hesitated. She had at first thought she should invite Joe in, but him stopping by this late in the evening to ask if she had found something in the attic to sell was odd. She wanted to end their conversation and go back to her dinner.

"I didn't find anything of value, Joe. I haven't really had a chance to think about the future or if I'm actually going to move or not. But, I do appreciate your offer if and when I do. I was just about to have dinner so you'll have to excuse me."

"Ok, Maria. I'll be happy to help you when you need it"

Joe turned around to walk away and when Maria was about to close the door he said with his back to her:

"Did you find any letters or photographs - you know the ones you thought your mother had brought over from Italy?"

"I did."

Joe turned around and looked at her with a cold, serious facial expression.

"Like the one photograph Harry said you had recognized"?

Maria didn't like the way Joe was staring at her.

"You know Joe I really need to get back in and finish my dinner before it gets cold"

"Oh, sure thing." Joe took a step forward and put his foot against the door just as Maria was ready to close it.

"Of course you should finish your dinner. I just need to know that the photograph is in safe hands. When you have more information about the family in the picture and who they may be I count on you letting me know."

Joe's foot was steadfast between the door and door frame, his eyes as dark as the night behind him. With a stern face and no sign of compassion or empathy for Maria, he waited for her response.

"Come by tomorrow morning first thing at my café and I'll tell you what I know, ok?" Maria said so Joe would leave. She with a gentle, but still determined push tried to close the door. Joe quickly moved his foot away, turned around and half-heartedly muttered an apology for stopping by so late in the evening.

Maria didn't hear it. She was too busy closing and locking the door. Joe's behavior was frightening and very different from what she, over the years, had found him to be; a rather odd but certainly not dangerous man with a past no one seemed to know anything about.

Maria picked up the phone and dialed Harry's number.

Chapter Twenty Five

Joe arrived ten minutes after Maria opened the café the following morning. Mrs. Rose had already left and Joe, who expected no one else to be there that early in the morning, was taken back upon seeing Harry by the counter sipping on his usual large latte with an extra shot of espresso.

"Hi Harry, you're up bright and early."

"I think that should be my line. What are you doing up so early Joe?"

"What can I get you Joe?" Maria interjected.

"Oh, just give me a regular cup of coffee please. Black, with three spoons of sugar."

Harry wrinkled his nose in disapproval.

"You know you are destroying not only a great cup of Maria's coffee but killing yourself prematurely with three spoons of sugar."

Joe would normally laugh it off and get back at Harry with a couple of playful jabs or comments. This time Joe didn't laugh, not even a smile.

Joe didn't like that Harry was there but wasn't about to wait for him to leave.

"I came over because Maria had asked me to stop by to talk about the picture Frank gave me."

"What about it?" Harry asked pretending he knew nothing about their conversation.

Joe decided to lay all his cards on the table.

"You know how Frank has been after me to find out more about the family in the picture I gave you? Since Maria has a copy of the same picture..."

Harry interrupted and looked at him with annoyance.

"Who told you Maria had a copy of the picture?"

"No one did, but Maria had mentioned to me the other day that she thought the picture was familiar. So you found it Maria?"

Harry turned to Joe and positioned himself right in front of him, only about ten inches away, looking down on the short, fat piece of shit as Frank always called him.

"Let me make this clear, Joe." Harry started off, "You asked me to find the Perugino family because Frank had asked you and I wanted to help you out. No one asked you to involve anyone else but me, and especially not Maria. Is that clear?"

Harry, now looking at the Joe he had gotten to know back in the correction center in LA, knew they had turned back the clock on their friendship to a time when Joe was over his head with problems. With the mob once more breathing down his neck Harry saw the fear in Joe's eyes.

"No more of this sneaking around my back, talking to Maria when the one you asked to help you was me, ok?" Harry continued with anger in his voice, using a body language not seen since his correction facility days. Both Joe and Maria looked at him with surprised and anxious faces.

"Ok, I get it, but get off my back now." Joe, having taken a few steps back, looked at Harry with anger and hatred – the same way he looked at Harry back at the correction center when they first met 30 years ago.

"Get out of here Joe. I will locate the Perugino family for you, for old time sakes, but keep away from Maria and me. And I would suggest you keep away from Frank as well."

Harry was furious and whatever odd friendship he and Joe had developed over the years was over. He knew, after this last favor, they would part ways. He couldn't have Joe's bad attitude, behavior and criminal background around Maria, negatively affecting his relationship with the one he really cared for. He was done with Joe, and felt no guilt letting him know; especially after all he had done for him over the years.

Joe muttered something, slammed the door behind him, and once he was back out on the street he smiled and said out loud:

"What was it Harry had said…the Perugino family…?"

With a smirk on his face he turned around, pleased with what he had found out.

Three days later, after Harry had found exactly what he was looking for; a record showing that yes, on July 17, 1945 a Perugino family of four had entered the U.S. through New York City harbor and the Ellis Island immigration facility, Maria and Harry were on their way to Italy on Alitalia Flight 609 to The Eternal City.

Somewhere over the Atlantic Ocean on route to Rome, Maria slept with her head resting on Harry's shoulder, who was looking at the picture. What he saw was a man and a woman, presumably the mother and father, with their three children, two boys and one girl.

One thing puzzled him though. Why did the records on Ellis Island only show four people with the name Perugino arriving that day on July 17, 1945 from Perugia, Italy?

Chapter Twenty Six

"Benevento a Roma."

The signs at the ultra-modern Leonardo da Vinci – Fiumicino Airport stood in sharp contrast with the backdrop of the Old Rome that Harry and Maria got a glimpse of when traveling on the fast speed Leonardo Airport Express train to Roma Termini, the main train station in Rome and the hub for the metro and city buses.

The train to Perugia was scheduled to depart in 30 minutes. Harry was used to travel light after his many photo journalist trips but Maria had a slightly different perception of traveling. For her, traveling light meant at least one large suitcase and carry on, enough for two weeks although the trip was only planned to last one.

The station was big but old and they realized they had arrived in the beautiful ancient city of Rome.

Struggling through the crowd of commuters and tourists they reached the ticket office service desk. Thinking they'd be better off getting personal service rather than using the ticket machines (they knew they had to switch trains and weren't sure where or when) they lined up to receive a number from a young, dark, tall, handsome looking but tired man, who seemed more interested in yawning and browsing internet on his phone than paying attention to Harry when he tried to explain in English where they were going and that they needed a customer service representative to help them find the right train and platform.

This was the first but soon to be followed by many more incidents during their week in Italy when Harry realized how much of a help Maria would be for him. He was excited to have her by his side for many reasons – the evenings and nights would be a lot more interesting than he was used to when traveling – and her knowledge of the Italian language wasn't limited to sex. It opened doors to most of Italy it seemed. The face of the young man lit up. The combination of a beautiful Signora and one who spoke the mother tongue woke him up from his boredom.

"Si, Signorina, Perugia. Vanno all'altezza dei finestrini e che vi aiuterà."

"What did he say?" Harry curiously asked Maria while smiling at the man who now had returned back to his internet browsing and tired looking face.

"He said a customer service representative at window eight would help us out."

Maria had already made way through the line with Harry following in her footsteps struggling with her suitcase, carry on and his own more modest back pack and small carry-on bag.

"Scouse, scouse" he said numerous times while the crowd parted way, muttering their disapproval how the tourists apparently got special treatment and were able to cut the line. The older, hunched back and gray haired overweight man in front of them looked up slowly from his screen that displayed all trains arriving and departing. It was a myriad of information and a miracle anyone could make any sense of all the numbers, times and flickering blimps indicating arriving trains in green and departing in red. The man took a look at Harry and quickly turned his attention to Maria with a smile on his face.

"Signora, come posso essere di servizio a voi?" His smile was exclusive for Maria because it quickly disappeared when he glanced over at Harry as if to confirm that "you have no clue to what I'm saying to your misses."

Maria, who obviously enjoyed both the attention she got and the fact she could practice the Italian she at this very moment was so grateful to her mother for teaching her, quickly got into a friendly conversation, making the old man's day. Both of them smiled and laughed while he with a few key strokes eliminated most of the clutter on his screen and replaced it with a couple of train options for Perugia. He pointed to a couple of them turning to Harry and in broken English explained that these four departures were their options – one leaving in 10 minutes from platform 2E (eastbound). They could make it if they hurried.

Tickets were printed and euros exchanged at a pace you wouldn't think was possible for a man of his demeanor, but when a language barrier is broken and a beautiful woman looks at you with a smile, miracles happen.

Harry and Maria walked fast, almost ran, to platform 2E that of course was in the opposite direction from the ticket office. When arriving about four minutes before departure and having to stand in line to validate the tickets – a procedure obviously more beneficial to keeping the unemployment numbers down than making the boarding of the trains more efficient – they realized that platform 2E was an extension of an already very long platform two. So with two minutes at hand they ran the 200 meters as if they were at the Colosseum back in the days when the slaves were running for their lives away from the starving lions.

Lucky to find two seats together they managed to fit their luggage on the shelf above – a very modern and clean train with comfortable seats. A nice surprise and contrast from the old train station with platforms that had seen their best days. Harry immediately connected his IPhone to the outlet next to his seat when Maria sighed loud and looked annoyed – but only for a second before her smile returned.

"What happened?" Harry asked wondering if it had something to do with an announcement he had just heard over the loudspeaker system.

"They just announced that the train is delayed ten minutes because of an incoming train on the track," Maria answered, leaned over and kissed Harry before he had a chance to react or say something. "That's life, could have been worse," she continued in her usual positive way, knowing very well that's a part of Italy she wouldn't miss when returning back home to Cold Spring.

The train ride to Perugia was going to take a little over two hours with a quick change in Foligno through what turned out to be the wonderful countryside of Umbria, whose Province of Perugia is its largest, covering two-thirds of the entire region. The ride, at sunset, turned out to be a spectacle of colors with the backdrop of the azure colored sky over the mountain slopes of the Apennines.

The commuters were busy with their smart phones, dozing off or reading a book or magazine. Soon Maria and Harry closed their eyes and when the sun set and the valleys with the small villages climbing up the mountain slope turned from day to night, they both were sleeping. Almost missing their connection they arrived in Perugia in the early evening of their first day and an adventure they had no idea would be a life changing week in more ways than one.

Chapter Twenty Seven

Harry was quick to hail a taxi outside the station. He had enough of carrying all the luggage and wasn't prepared to climb the hill up to the old city of Perugia after a long trip. Not getting much sleep on the plane ride from New York and only an hour or so on the train from Rome to Perugia they were both ready for bed but not before having a bite to eat – something they also completely forgot about over the last very busy twenty four hours of traveling across the Atlantic.

After what wasn't a long trip in miles but very curvy, narrow and frightening in and out of narrow streets not even wide enough to fit a little Fiat, the large taxi suddenly made a sharp turn to avoid a terrified pedestrian who barely escaped being run over by the taxi. The driver jumped out, said a few words to the now not only terrified but also angry pedestrian, and announced to Maria that this is where he needed to stop, pointing a few meters down the road to where Hotel Anna was located.

Fifteen euros later, Harry and Maria looked at each other, baffled but now wide awake after the furious roller coaster ride, wondering where the entrance to the Anna Hotel was. The driver noticed their surprised looks and pointed towards a huge iron door that seemed more likely to be the entrance to a medieval castle than to a hotel. A small sign next to a buzzer did confirm that they had reached their destination. The door was locked but even before they had a chance to buzz the hotel a man came over to open the door with one of his keys, letting Harry and Maria in, explaining that the hotel was on the second floor.

It was called a hotel but it was really an Inn. A place Harry had quickly found when making the hasty preparations for their trip and stay in Perugia. With good reviews and comments about the friendly old couple running it, Harry thought it was just the right place for he and Maria to spend time together and enjoy the surrounding restaurants in the best place in town – the old city center – Centro di Perugia.

Signore and Signora Catalano were both waiting for Harry and Maria when they entered the Inn located in an apartment building on the second floor and the lobby that used to be a hallway.

"Buena sera," Signora Catalano said with a big smile. At little more than five feet tall, a few pounds extra pasta weight, gray haired and a face with a few wrinkles she had seen a hard but happy life passing by.

Working out of their home at their age was not only very convenient but allowed them the time they needed in between to spend time together.

Signore Catalano was as short, if not even shorter than his wife and with that same big smile and friendly face they were a perfect hostess and host. His glasses hanging down to his nose tip, his round friendly face, cheeks red from his daily wine intake and when walking down the hallway dragging his feet after him, reminded Harry about how perfect this nice, friendly Italian gentleman could have been as Santa at Macy's.

"Prego." he said with obvious pride in his voice, offering their best room, number six, for the beautiful Signora Maria and the handsome Signore Harry.

"Molto Bueno." Maria replied when she saw the simple, but large and clean, richly decorated room. It seemed like the perfect fit for how she imagined someone's home in Italy.

"Ah, the view; It's magnificent," she continued and quickly translated it into Italian for the old man who smiled an even larger smile.

They quickly decided they must have the best view of the Inn overlooking the rooftops of Perugia and down the valley with the lights from both the old city and the area down the valley sparkling like stars in the sky.

Harry had already looked up a nearby restaurant on his iPhone. Del Bongo on nearby Via Della Sosa was a short ten minutes or less walk from Anna Hotel and had received great reviews as one of the better restaurants in all Perugia. Seemed like a perfect fit for Harry and when he suggested it to Maria she quickly accepted his invitation. They were both hungry and tired and wanted to eat, go to bed and wake up next to each other the following morning at sunrise in their room with a view.

Soon they were sitting at what would become their restaurant for the whole week. Every evening they showed up they got the same table, got to know the owners, waiter and of course got to try most of the delicious dishes on the menu.

It was a very cozy, family oriented restaurant that besides the charming ambiance served the very best local cuisine. Old vaulted ceilings in the downstairs area of the restaurant and a small bar and a few tables on the street level made it one of the smallest yet still one of the most popular restaurants in the area. The white cellar walls, the sturdy solid wood tables and chairs gave it a rustic look Harry imagined an Italian country-house somewhere in Umbria away from the city would look like.

The drawings on the walls were of local scenes, as customary in most Italian restaurants. The pride of family and neighborhood means something to this part of the world, Harry thought to himself when pulling out the chair for Maria once the friendly waiter showed them to their table for two in the downstairs dining area.

The candle was flickering its friendly light and Harry took a moment to look into Maria's eyes. He smiled and said the words he hadn't said in a long time:

"I love you, Maria."

Maria took a while to respond but her eyes and smile gave it away, before she spoke. Her lips sensual, exciting and inviting; her face beautifully shining in the light of the candle; and her eyes tearing up.

"I love you too, Harry. And I'm happy beyond anything to be here with you, in this city where my mother was raised and lived. I'm so excited to find out more about my relatives, to meet my niece who should still live here but more so than anything, to be able to share it with you."

Harry didn't have to reply. He continued to look Maria in the eyes, smiled and leaned over the table to kiss her.

"Let's order," he said after tasting the love from Maria's lips. They had done its magic to Harry's appetite for more.

"We are both tired and the bed back at the hotel appeals to me right now in more ways than one." he continued with a wink of an eye.

Maria gave up a laugh, reached out to hold Harry's hand who willingly let her touch him. Maria crossed her legs under the table although the urge to open them were stronger. Harry used his free hand to reach under the table; finding the opening in Maria's dress he was looking for; letting his hand wander off along the inner thigh of Maria's left leg – the one she had positioned on top of her right when crossing them. He didn't move his eyes from hers and it wasn't until she closed them and the pointed tip of her tongue touched her upper lip and her face blushed, not of embarrassment but of excitement, that Harry stopped his move up her thigh. Maria opened her eyes in disappointment just as the waiter arrived.

"Cosa posso fare per te?" he asked turning to Maria who placed her order for insalata mista for an appetizer and aubergine and pesto ravioli for her entre.

She ordered, in perfect Italian, Harry's choice of assorted cured meat as an appetizer and filet of beef as his choice of main dish. After half a liter of vino rosso, lemon sorbet, espresso and grappa they paid; left for their 10 minutes stroll through the narrow and beautifully lit streets of the old city of Perugia; struggling with the heavy medieval entrance door to their Hotel Anna; before litteraly jumping into bed for some well deserved rest and sleep.

Their first night in Perugia, Italy, was a night to remember.

Chapter Twenty Eight

In all the excitement, their tired bodies hadn't closed the window shutters. They both woke up at sunrise and while Harry went into the bathroom, Maria took the sheet, wrapped it around her naked body and stood up in front of the window with a view over the rooftops, the valley and the Apennines majestically covered in the morning fog the sun desperately was trying to break through. Without thinking Maria raised her arms in the air to stretch and to fully embrace the beauty.

The sheet, as in slow motion, fell to the floor at the same time Harry came out from the bathroom, as naked as God had created him. He went over to Maria with her hands still in the air, taking in the beautiful scene in front of her.

Harry took in a different view. He focused in on Maria's beautiful naked body, thinking how lucky he was to have found love at last. He put his hands on Maria's hip and surprised by the touch Maria turned around, her face right at Harry's hairy chest. She leaned forward, buried her face in his chest and started kissing his nipples the way she knew he liked. Soon Harry's hands eagerly touched Maria's soft skin, finding their way up to her face and gently moved her head away from his chest and positioned his lips close to hers as to just get a taste of what he had missed out on.

The kiss was passionate, yet gentle and more sensual than sexual. It woke up all their senses though and soon they were engaged with Harry sitting on the chair by the wide open window awaiting the arrival of Maria who was slowly but accurately moving her body in a position to lock the two of them together. Deep inside of her Harry and Maria rhythmically and with the precision of a drummers' beat worked up to a crescendo that made Maria moan out loud in the early morning and in front of other early risers in Perugia.

Happily, they fell asleep in each other's arms for another hour before they woke up to the sound of their host and hostess preparing breakfast in the area across from their room.

The breakfast was served in the old dining room next to the kitchen, decorated with dollhouse precision and filled with Signora Catalano's passion for ceramics and porcelain trinkets. Everything from ballerinas in fine porcelain to Santa souvenir figurines mass produced in China and competing for the limited space left along the walls.

Café-size table seating arrangements gave away the fact that this place was for couples in love looking for an unusual but secluded way of getting lost, not only in this intimate dining area but in the narrow streets of the old city of Perugia.

The espresso was as strong and delicious as could be expected; the home made rolls and cakes just perfect; and the cornetto with preserves fresh as if they just came out of the oven. The Café Americana was equally strong

163

and delicious. Harry and Maria took their time and when some of the other guests had finished and left, Signora Catalano, or Anna as she preferred Maria to address her, came in to chat with Maria. Harry was just finishing up his first cup of Café Americana and was heading over to the espresso machine for a double, when Maria took out the photograph of the Perugina family from her bag and showed it to Anna.

Harry could only silently sit and watch Maria and Anna's conversation that, at one point, became very animated. They were both talking at the same time; finishing each other's sentences; names were flying back and forth and suddenly Anna started clapping her hands in excitement, arose from her chair and hugged Maria while tears of happiness rolled down her cheeks. Maria, looked over at Harry to acknowledge that she had something to say to him but it had to wait because there was no way of stopping Anna from talking.

Bursting of excitement, Harry realized that there had been a, sudden and welcome, breakthrough in the mystery of the photograph – or at least a recognition and a familiarity with the Perugino family in the picture. He could hear the names Franco, Rachel, Angelina, Eduardo and Leonardo mentioned many times and also what appeared to be Maria's mom's name Francesca.

When, after what felt like an eternity for Harry, Anna finally got up to attend to some other guests who had arrived for a late breakfast, he could ask Maria about what was said during Anna and her long conversation.

"So, tell me, what did she say." Harry asked, as he exploded in curiosity, and couldn't wait another second to hear what Maria had found out.

"Well, it's amazing how lucky we are staying at this hotel" Maria said with an undertone of meaning both the sex and the fact that they both were here to locate some family members – in Maria's case her own and in Harry's the relatives in the picture.

"I know. Tell me more."

"Anna, that is Signora Catalono and her family, knew my family AND the Perugino family. It's an amazing coincidence but it sounds like my mother somehow was involved with the Perugino family and I also know that you have come to the right place. Leonardo Perugino, the oldest son in the picture has been living here for many years and although keeping a very low profile, has a successful vineyard just outside the city. I can't believe the luck we are having but I guess the expression when it rains it pours is very much true for us right now."

Maria gave Harry one of her big smiles and with a wink of her eye she declared that she loved it when it poured.

"Oh, Maria, thank you for being here with me – I mean, you know what I mean,"

Harry was so excited about the news and how they had literally stumbled on this information on the second day of their stay – well, really, first morning after arrival the night before, that he, in a rather un-Harry like way grabbed Maria, and with no hesitation kissed her right there in the middle of the breakfast room. Anna turned around after having served some coffee to the guests that just arrived, smiled at them both, throwing both of her arms up in the air and expressed what they all felt at this very moment:

"Belissimo."

Chapter Twenty Nine

The following day, they headed over to the vineyard of Leonardo Perugino and met the man in the picture. Thanks to Maria, her charm and connection to the Perugino family and the region, they got his attention.

Leonardo decided, despite the many years he kept his life a secret, to open up about his past. He realized, after keeping it all inside behind a wall of silence, that by telling his side of the story he could free himself from the heavy burden he had carried around all these years.

Over the next couple of days, Harry met with Leonardo alone, while Maria was busy locating and meeting with her relatives that Leonardo helped her find. On their third day in Perugia, Maria again accompanied Harry to see Leonardo.

"Signora Cammeresi, please come in. Have a glass of my wine." Leonardo completely ignored Harry. Ever since he met Maria the first time and found out she was the daughter of Francesca who baby sat his little brother Eduardo back then, Leonardo had eyes for Maria only.

"Signor Perugino, I'd love to have a glass of your wonderful Chianti" Maria answered. Harry took his usual position next to Leonardo at the table.

"Signora, did you find your mother's niece who lives down by the bus station?"

"Signor Perugino, I did and I'm so happy for your help. It was "fantastico" to meet her and to get to know

167

my Aunt and through her how close my mother was with her sister. If it wasn't for you Signor Perugino I would never have met any of my relatives here in Italy and hear their stories about my "famiglia."

Ever since Maria was introduced to Leonardo, it was like the switch had been turned on and there was nothing Leonardo didn't want to talk about. Harry knew then that bringing Maria with him to Italy wasn't just very lovely and exciting for him, but essential in getting Leonardo to tell his story – the one that he came for and that, for whatever it was worth at this point, Joe and Frank wanted to know.

Leonardo, a now 89-year-old man, was born in Perugia in 1926.

Perugia, the capital city of Umbria in central Italy, only a couple of hours train ride from Rome, had, just like Leonardo, not changed much over the years.

Once a tall dark, handsome, man, Leonardo still knew how to charm a woman. His very manly and stern face with eyes that seemed to change colors with the mood he was in, was evidence of a man who had been through a lot. His arrogant and superior way of thinking about himself as the only real man around stood in sharp contrast to a very soft and much more sensitive side of him that became known to only a few. Over the course of Harry and Maria's meetings with him, it became obvious that this was a man who had not only been through a lot, but who needed to tell his story; a story he hadn't told anyone; a story he had kept secret for his own family over the last sixty years after his return to Italy in 1953.

Leonardo was thrilled to see Maria and more than willing to share his life with Harry, the man Maria was in love with and who Leonardo immediately found both charming and interesting. He saw something of himself in Harry – thirty two years younger when he himself was fifty seven. How he wished he could have met Francesca, the same way Harry had been fortunate enough to meet Maria, his teenage sweetheart, after years of waiting.

Leonardo had run his vineyard into a rather successful business over the years since returning from the States. Enjoying a comfortable but lonely life, the vineyard was run by his manager, a trusted local who had been a friend of Leonardo's aunt on his mother's side. The success of the vineyard meant Leonardo could hire all the people he needed to run it without his daily involvement. It had been like that for many of the last 10 years. He would be first to admit that he had lived comfortably for a Perugia resident, a rather luxurious lifestyle. Still it was a very lonely way of spending your last years.

He was now ready to share the story that had kept him in Perugia, like a hostage in his own home, for the last sixty years.

Harry had so far only gotten a vague idea about Leonardo's past. Ever since Maria was introduced, Leonardo seemed stuck repeating the details around the wonderful days when Francesca was there to baby sit. Leonardo, at the time already a teenager himself, had a secret crush on Maria's mother who was a couple of years younger than him.

Later, Harry would realize that when Francesca was there to babysit, it was a reminder of a situation that seemed to cast a love "spell" on a time in life that was far from the past.

"So, Mr. Perugino, should we continue our story from the time you started working at the local bakery at the age of 16 back in 1942?"

Leonardo seemed annoyed but as long as he could keep his eyes on Maria, the daughter of his secret crush back then he was more than willing to tell Harry the story about how he came to leave Italy in 1944, only to find himself returning in 1953 after only eight years in the U.S. Years that would define who he would become and why he, for the last sixty years, had lived a quiet life back in his home town of Perugia. It turned out to be a direct result of what happened to him in New York City.

"Like I've already told you Signor Anderson," Leonardo obviously not happy to leave the more pleasant memories of Maria's mother behind, continued with his story about how he at age sixteen, and after finishing school, started working at the bakery down the street.

"It was hard work. Long hours and then of course when my day was over I got back home just in time to say goodbye to Francesca and to take care of my little sister and brother." Leonardo paused.

"Signor Perugino, did you ever get a chance to spend any other time with my mother?" Maria interrupted the silence that had followed. She had figured that Leonardo had a teenage crush on her mother at the time and was curious to know if they got an opportunity to date.

Leonardo's face turned from a grim one thinking about his hard and long working hours at the bakery, to a smile when his thoughts went back to Francesca and the one time they went to the movies.

"Si, we were able to take off one evening." Leonardo's face lit up and he again seemed to be lost in his past.

"Signor Perugino, you had mentioned to me the other day," Harry interrupted, "that you never really saw your father."

Harry thought it best to move things along and not get caught up in a teenage love affair. As interesting as it may be for Maria, he wanted to move on and find out more about Leonardo's family and the reasons for them coming to America.

Leonardo turned towards Harry, looked him straight in his eyes and casually continued:

"My father's only way of showing his appreciation for my mother and what she did for us, was to beat and rape her."

Leonardo, with a hard yet emotional stare, didn't say more. Harry and Maria looked at each other in shock. The silence that followed was painful. Leonardo hadn't had the best of childhoods and Maria's mother Francesca, unaware of the disturbing scenes taking place in the same house she so often visited, had probably spread more joy than she could ever have imagined in a household tainted by domestic violence.

Maria excused herself, telling Leonardo she had an appointment with her niece. She nodded at Harry who knew she needed some fresh air. It reminded her of how her abusive husband Robert, just over a month ago, had threatened to rape her, before his accidental, but liberating, death.

Chapter Thirty

"I want to tell you about my years in New York now" Leonardo continued once Maria had said her goodbyes, giving them both, as custom is, two loving kisses on their cheeks.

"The sun." Leonardo gazed up to the ceiling as if he could see the sun up there.

"The sun made the harbor in New York glitter that day. It welcomed us and made us feel at home. The trip from Marseille was long and the boat that took us over was just a small liner that went back and forth from port to port once Marseille was liberated."

"Marseille you said Signor?"

"Yes that's what I said wasn't it."

Leonardo lost his patience and got irritated when having to repeat himself. Harry wasn't going to push it. He just made a note to get back to why Marseille, when Leonardo was ready to talk about his years growing up and leaving Italy.

"Where was I? Oh, si, we passed by the Statue of Liberty and I remember my mother crying." Leonardo's story came to a halt again. Harry started to wonder how much time it would take for Leonardo to tell his whole story. Maria had to go back in one week's time. At this pace Harry was afraid they wouldn't get to the end of Leonardo's life story until next month.

"Did you pass through Ellis Island and what happened after that, Signor Perugino?" Harry's attempt to speed things up was met with an annoyed glance from Leonardo and Harry decided to slow down to the pace of the story and focus on what Leonardo had to say, even when pausing to reflect. This conversation couldn't be rushed. Even if it would take two weeks or more, Harry would be there for the whole journey. Patience, he thought to himself, will pay off. Leonardo's story was going to be a fascinating one, of that he was certain.

"My mother's cousin who had moved to New York back in the 20's met us and drove us to their home in the Bronx, a home that turned out to be ours too for a couple of years. You see, all housing complexes throughout the city were either built for or occupied by returning soldiers and their families."

"July 17, 1945. That day is forever in my mind. We all thought it was going to be the beginning of a new life. It was in many ways. We had left the land of limitations to arrive to the land of opportunity."

"You know Signor Anderson, my mother was a Jew."

Harry was taken by surprise by this news. It was said in a way that implied hardship but at this point he wasn't sure if Leonardo related it to hardship in the land of limitations they had left or hardship in their new land of opportunity. Harry again decided not to probe but wait for

174

an explanation later, when Leonardo chose to tell him more.

"And you know, she cried on September 8, that year, when Miss America was crowned in Atlantic City. She was chosen by returning soldiers who had been prisoners of war in Germany. She was a Bronx girl. Her name was, I remember it as if it was yesterday, Bess Myerson. She was a Jew."

"What was your mother's name?"

"Her name was Rachel Perugino. She was a loving mother and took good care of us. Her cousin's family was Catholic and so were we, even if my mother was born a Jew. She was still very proud when our first Miss America was a Jew."

Again, Harry was curious about Leonardo's Jewish background but could only assume Rachel, his mother, married into a catholic family back in Italy. He decided not to interrupt Leonardo but instead make another mental note.

"So, we were very lucky. We had a home, relatives who invited us with open arms, and a future filled with opportunities." Leonardo paused again, his face turned stern and serious after showing a softer side of him, talking about his mother.

"I was only 19. And I was sent there to work for the mob."

Chapter Thirty One

Harry looked up from his notes, glanced over at the man in front of him.

"The mob?" he repeated quietly as if to convince himself that he hadn't misunderstood Leonardo.

"Si, la mafia."

Leonardo, the quiet man in front of him had spent the many years in the small sleepy town of Perugia, taking care of his successful vineyard. Looking fragile but still mentally very sharp, he sat with a straight back behind a desk that was as old as he was. A heavy piece of oak furniture as intrinsic looking as Leonardo's mind. Harry thought about the The Godfather and imagined Leonardo as Don Perugino running his family business with an iron fist behind the desk, making all these decisions about who should live and who should die. Harry's mind quickly returned to reality when Leonardo continued:

"Well, Signor Anderson," as if he knew what Harry was thinking, "as a non -Sicilian I was never a member of the mafia. I had been sent over by the mob in Marseille to make the necessary connections with the New York City crime families."

"During our time in Marseille," he continued, "we lived with a French professor of English, Alain, who successfully helped at least twenty other Italian Jews from being deported by the Germans. They felt he was useful

176

because of his language skills and I think they looked the other way a few times."

"He also taught my family English which of course was very helpful once we got to New York in 1945."

"How did you get involved with the French mob?" Harry quickly asked to avoid getting off track again.

"You see, Signor Anderson, what could a refugee family do while not speaking the language or knowing the French ways? You do it by constantly hiding and looking over your shoulder to avoid being caught by the Germans. We needed to find ways to repay our friend Alain, even if he never asked for anything in return. Such a good man he was."

Leonardo paused.

It was in these moments Harry saw something in Leonardo that he didn't imagine possible for a man who must have had a very rough and violent past. The compassion, the empathy and softness seemed to play a much larger role in his life than what normally he associated with the mob. Maybe it was the many years he had spent in Italy after returning back from the States that had softened him, or possibly an innate goodness that could never be completely deflated.

He was a very interesting character and Harry couldn't wait to hear more of his story as it developed.

"It was just an easy way to make some good money. And the mob protected us. "No one asked any questions. Alain was too busy working on his cover up. I needed to take care of my family."

"Drugs?" Harry asked, knowing how well connected the French mob was at the time with the suppliers in the Middle East. With Marseille being one of the largest and least controlled ports in Europe during the War, it was a gold mine with huge profits and low risks if you were well connected.

"Si, Signor Anderson. Drugs. So easy and with no restrictions a gold mine for the French to set up their operation in New York. I was nineteen, and it was the ticket for my family to come to the States and our relatives there."

Again, Leonardo paused.

Harry looked up, his face not more than two feet away from Leonardo's. Their eyes met and Harry shivered despite the unseasonable hot and humid weather Perugia had offered them upon arriving from Rome a couple of days ago.

The tall, tired looking man looked nothing like the mobster he once was, except for the eyes. They were ice cold with no mercy and lacked all the compassion, empathy and softness they had previously radiated. Harry hadn't, until now, considered that right next to him, sitting behind that large, old desk was a man with a lengthy criminal past. One who wouldn't make any excuses for the string of victims he had left behind suffering; feeding the drug addicts the poison they needed to survive another day while safeguarding the survival of his own family with the money he collected.

Harry saw the danger in Leonardo's eyes and even if it was thanks to Maria that Harry had gotten this once in a lifetime sit down with a mobster he wondered what he had gotten into with Maria.

"I'm getting tired Signor Anderson. I need to get something to eat and go to sleep."

When looking up again, Harry found himself staring into Leonardo's ice cold eyes.

"Just wondering though. I know why Maria is here but what's your interest in my story, Signor Anderson?"

Leonardo's eyes burned like fire. Harry, eager to not yet end their conversation for the day, realized that Leonardo was about to stop talking about his past, decided it was time to mention more than just the old picture of his family he had showed Leonardo the first time they met two days ago.

"Signor Perugino," Harry started saying when Leonardo raised a hand to stop him.

"Signor Anderson, please call me Leo and I'll call you Harry." Still staring at Harry he continued, "I'm telling you my story because I want to, but with one condition."

There was a long pause.

"There are going to be some things I'd rather you don't repeat to anyone, and especially not to Maria."

Harry took a deep breath, relieved that Leonardo still wanted to tell his story and that he didn't have to say more, at this point, about Joe and Frank and the unknown reasons for their interest in Leonardo and his family. Thankfully, he either forgot or decided not to follow up his question as to why Harry was so very interested in his story.

"I understand, Leo. I won't tell Maria about anything you don't want her to know."

"Good. Let's stop here for today. Go and have dinner with your beautiful fidanzata and we will continue tomorrow."

Harry was relieved to leave. He couldn't wait to see Maria for a romantic dinner and not having to stare into those fiery eyes of Leonardo any longer.

Chapter Thirty Two

"I love you," Harry whispered, his tongue playing with Maria's ear.

Her breathing and heart beat increased at the pace of Harry's rhythmic, loving and passionate movements.

"Oh, don't stop," she screamed out, looking deep into his eyes as he moved inside her. Tears of joy streamed down her face.

"So good," she screamed, holding on to the bed frame that was banging hard against the wall.

"Don't stop, Maria. Harry's body stiffened, as hard as his penis. He let it all out, leaving nothing behind, giving her all of him.

Looking deep into each other's eyes they opened up their souls and hearts to each other. There was no need for interpretation. Her wide open lust-filled eyes didn't only satisfy their sexual appetite for each other but displayed a stronger commitment than any spoken vows. The raw yet sensitive, bold yet gentle and free spirited sex took them to another place, time and age. Without saying a single word, their eyes and adoring looks left them breathless, and very satisfied.

Harry broke the magical silence.

"Maria, I love you for not only who you are, but for what I am when I am with you." Harry turned over, his lips close to hers without touching them.

Maria kissed him gently, smiled and whispered in his ear. "You always had a way with words. I l love you Harry" She got up, stretched her body, her nipples hard and inviting for Harry to see.

"Are you hungry, my love," she asked in a sexy tone, licking her finger, suggesting she wasn't done yet. She didn't wait for Harry's answer. "I am, and I can't wait to eat," she said, putting her whole finger in her mouth. Harry jumped out of bed and playfully ran after her into the shower.

The water streaming down on their naked bodies, Maria started kissing Harry's chest. Moving down she took him all in. They were as bold as they once were back in high school and they enjoyed every minute of their newfound and playful love.

"So should we go back to Del Borgo?" Harry asked as they strolled down the old and narrow city streets of Perugia, the home of the Baci chocolate factory and the University attended by many international students.

"Yes, let's do that." Maria was hungry and it seemed like Del Borgo Ristorante had become their restaurant of choice for their stay in Perugia.

The streets were crowded with students and tourists. The locals were having their family dinners, and wide open windows exposed the warm and balmy temperature of the evening. Maria and Harry saw and heard them eat, laugh and enjoy heated conversations about everything from sports to politics.

The owners at Del Borgo Ristorante greeted them with the charming Italian hospitality one would expect from a small family-owned restaurant. As Harry and Maria returned for yet another meal, the owners realized Maria was of Italian decent when she started speaking Italian to them. She was then treated as if she was part of the family.

Alessia, the wife, and chef, came out of the kitchen to explain that the cured meat she had picked up at the market earlier in the day was out of this world. Her daughter, Anjelica, busy serving other guests, took the time to pay special attention to Maria and Harry. When the owner, Edmondo, the head of the family, came out to serve the Chianti, he made sure to stay by their table for a long time, listening to Maria's story of her family growing up right here in Perugia.

"Thank you," Maria grabbed Harry's hand when they left the restaurant after four hours of dining, drinking and talking. They were miles away from Cold Springs and only a couple of weeks into finding their way back to each other. Everything between them happened at the speed of light. Their love was bold and pure; their commitment was solid and their passion fiery. They were truly in love.

They fell asleep in each other's arms; the open window allowed the evening breeze to cool them. Outside on the street by the entrance to Albergo Anna, a man leaned casually against the lamp post, smoking a cigarette. He would stay there watching their window for the rest of the night.

Chapter Thirty Three

Harry left Maria still asleep in bed with the windows still open and honking horns now blared from the Fiats traveling down the impossibly narrow streets. Harry caught himself pondering as he left their lovely Anna Inn with Mrs. Catalano's loud "Bongiorno" still ringing in his ears.

"How can she sleep through all the noise?" he said to himself while he narrowly escaped being run over by a Fiat whose owner said some well-chosen words in Italian to him.

"Screw you," he screamed back in English.

Harry couldn't believe what he just said, but there was something about the intensity and the passion of the people he had met over the last couple of days that sparked a newfound passion in him as well. He was also grateful that Maria was the recipient of this passion. It was not only a refreshing change from the much more "controlled" Cold Spring. As he normally travelled alone, having someone to share his impressions and passion with, was a wonderful treat.

Harry strolled down the street to find the taxi that for some reason always seemed to be standing there, right around the corner from Albergo Anna. It seemed the driver never had any other customers than the guests staying at the Inn. Harry got into the back seat, and asked to be driven to the Perugino Vineyard, only 10km south of the old city.

It was another beautiful morning and the drive a very scenic one. Today was the first time Harry paid attention to the many long lines of grapes growing on both sides of the narrow dirt road leading to the vineyard.

The Perugino Vineyard was one of the most successful in the region and Leonardo had run it ever since he came back. Now it practically ran itself with the help of people Leonardo trusted and who for generations had worked for him. It was truly a family run business with employees beginning with the very young, whose first job was the same first job as their fathers, mothers, grandfathers and grandmothers. Leonardo referred to them not as employees, but family members.

"Bongiorno, Harry. Have a glass of wine. Sit down. I'll tell you about how I made my first contacts in New York."

Harry poured Leonardo a glass of wine and one for himself, although it was only ten o'clock in the morning.

"Grazie amico mio."

Even with the very limited Italian Harry had picked up over the last couple of days from Maria, he knew that having Leonardo calling him his friend meant a lot.

"But first, Harry, I need to ask you something we didn't finish."

Harry found himself staring into the same blazing eyes he had been so relieved to leave behind yesterday.

Leonardo leaned forward, motioning for Harry to move closer.

He wasn't asking Harry; he was commanding him to get closer. Leonardo was used to get what he wanted. His charm and care for his family stood in sharp contrast to the calculating, demanding and frightening way he dominated conversations. Leonardo whispered to Harry, who was now only inches away from Leonardo's searing eyes.

"Why are you here?"

Harry leaned back and looked down so as to avoid facing Leonardo while lying to him about his reasons for traveling halfway around the world to locate an 89-year-old former mobster. Here was that question he had avoided answering the day before. This time he had to provide an explanation.

"I live in a small town north of New York City; the same town where Maria grew up."

Still looking down, he continued;

"I found the photograph I gave you the other day, in an antique store in town. I was intrigued by it, and Maria by a strange coincidence, found the same photograph while cleaning up in her attic."

Harry looked up again and remarked, "I am a photojournalist and I love to travel."

Leonardo stood up from his chair behind the desk and once again was mere inches away from Harry. He put his right hand on Harry's left shoulder, leaned over and whispered into his ear;

"I will tell you a story I never told anyone before, not even my own famiglia."

Chapter Thirty Four

Harry's life was about to change but he had no idea how much it would affect him. He was ready to hear the story of a man, who at eighteen, felt obliged to make a decision he could not tell anyone, not even, and especially not, his own family.

Until recently, when Leonardo was reminded about his past as a ruthless mobster, he thought his story would die with him. But all that changed in a heartbeat. It wasn't because of Harry and his plan to write the whole story for The New York Times, a newspaper he had worked very closely with as a freelance photojournalist.

Instead it was his teenage love story in the 1940's with Maria's mom, the babysitter of his little brother and sister, that had made him realize it was time for the truth to come out and for his family to know what really had happened back in Italy, Marseille and New York before his sudden and without any trace disappearance in 1953. His decisions and sacrifices he made over the years were for the sake of them and their future wellbeing. The family he so delicately kept in the dark about his criminal activities, the murder and violence he had been involved in ever since Marseille, was necessary to do. He did it all for them, to be safe and live the American Dream.

For him, over the years, only one thing had mattered. How to best protect his family from the tragic truth they knew nothing about. To sacrifice his own happiness was the price he'd paid. Did he regret having done what he did? Of course the hardship of having to cut the ties with his family, never to hear from them or them from him, was a huge burden to carry throughout his life. Their success depended on his making the decision he made in 1953 when leaving the US, and to find himself back in his hometown of Perugia. He had left his family in the hands of others who had sworn to keep them safe. Over the sixty years that followed he had received sporadic reports about the family and Rachel, his mother, whose funeral he had not been able to attend. His little brother, living in Florida after a successful career in banking and his sister, who he back then had done so much to protect, now a successful therapist with her own practice.

Of course he would have preferred another outcome. At the time, no other alternative existed when Leonardo made the decision to bring his family to safety. What followed was a path of survival, more so for his mother, brother and sister, than for himself. Despite the very tumultuous life he had lived ever since arriving to Marseille and up to his disappearance in 1953, he never thought about his choices being anything but necessary to protect the ones he loved.

Decisions made that would benefit and keep his family safe were the easy ones to make. To have to lie to everyone he loved and not being able to tell his side of the story, was the hard part, and what finally made him decide to reveal the truth.

To tell his story to Maria, the daughter of his teenage love and Harry, the man sitting right in front of him and who he identified himself with and thought he could have become under different circumstances, felt like the right thing to do. Leonardo saw in Harry a man who had become someone he never could be. Living his dreams of an adventurous life, without having to kill; finding love without having to force himself on it; free and not chained to a past, a prisoner of circumstances he had no control over.

He had finally found his audience. A secret kept for over sixty years. A life he never expected to live to tell; a story he never felt had to be told but one he had to share beyond the quiet town of Perugia and the hills of Umbria.

Unaware that the events actually had shaped history, he was eager to share his life from the war stricken Italy in the 1940s, his involvement in the rising and highly profitable drug trafficking from the Middle East via Marseille and his assignment to set up the operation for the drug trafficking in New York City.

This was the story about the life and fate of the Perugino family, one of many mobster families in the 1940s and 50s. This though, was a family who never knew how they were cared for. His mother, little brother and sister thought the whole time that Leonardo's work was legitimate and honest income from the import business from Marseille. The guilt of having deceived and hidden the truth from them, which was necessary to survive, was one he now could put behind him. The truth, as fascinating as it was to millions of readers who would get a glimpse into the secret world of a mobster, would, and even more importantly, be known to his family.

"Let me start with when we arrived to Marseille," Leonardo said, sipping on his wine.

"Why did you move to Marseille?" Harry looked up from his notebook after the silence that followed. Leonardo looked at him with a stern, unfriendly face. His eyes stared at Harry. Sharp as knives and with surgical precision they found the soft spots and Harry, uncomfortable, retreated by lowering his head in sadness. Sitting behind the old oak desk was a ruthless former mobster who didn't expect to answer any questions.

He expected to run the show, ask all the questions and answer them, when and if he wanted to.

Harry by now had realized this wasn't going to be an interview. No words were spoken. Leonardo's eyes said it all. Harry knew this was a one of a kind opportunity to write an article about a man and his story no one had heard before, not even his own family. Harry was hopeful, excited and full of anticipation of putting together an article that may very well be the best, most interesting and captivating report he'd ever done before.

This one will ignite my rather long dry spell of unpublished attempts, he thought to himself before Leonardo once more took command and continued:

"We, my mother, brother, sister and I arrived to Marseille in July of 1944, at a time when the Allied forces rapidly were approaching Perugia and the Germans retreating up north, leaving a string of violence, rapes and killings behind. We just escaped in time."

Leonardo sat quietly, close to tears in the same, but now emphatic eyes that a minute ago had stared down Harry with such knife sharp determination and vigor.

It gave Harry time to reflect on what Leonardo had just told him. Why Marseille and why did he only mention arriving with his mom, brother and sister? Did his father stay behind? Knowing he could not ask any questions, he looked up at Leonardo, as to try and read his intention. Was that a tear Leonardo just wiped off his left eye? It was and leaving Perugia for Marseille, even after nearly seventy years, apparently hit a nerve with the hardnosed former mobster.

"We left with only what we could carry with us. My mother had a cousin who a couple of weeks earlier had decided it was time to leave. The day before we left with them, my father disappeared."

Leonardo paused for a brief moment. Did I see a smile on his face, Harry thought. He remembered that Leonardo the other day had told him about the abusive side of his father who didn't seem to care about anything but himself.

"We feared for our lives. You see, Harry, like I told you the other day, my mother was Jewish. My father was a Nazi collaborator."

Silence followed the statement that brought back the terrible images of Jews being deported, and even if Italian catholic families helped many to hide, there were tens of thousands of Jews who were unable to escape the terrible fate history had wrought upon them. And at a time when Italy was as divided as ever with the Allies moving up from Sicily, the Italian communist partisans fighting German appointed Mussolini's marionette government in the Northern Italy. That part of Italy was still occupied and controlled by the Germans despite the decision by the Italian King in July 1943 to assign Pietro Badoglio as head of a military government, declaring war with Germany a year before Leonardo and family decided to flee to Marseille.

Leonardo lowered his head, as if to show respect to his mother Rachel. Harry didn't move, looking at Leonardo, trying to anticipate what was coming next. Leonardo looked up. This time he showed a very different side of him. He looked angry, hateful and with a stern look on his face continued:

"The bastard was going to give up his own wife, my mother, and bring his children with him up north to join the Germans."

Leonardo, with remarkable strength for a 90 year old, slammed his right fist on the old oak desk in front of him with such vigor Harry could have sworn he saw the desk move.

"There was nothing I could do other than make the man who was supposed to protect his family, and not give them up, pay for his actions."

Harry wondered in what way but before he had any chance to think more about it, Leonardo continued:

"So, I decided the only thing I could do was to take charge of the family, being the eldest. So in all haste we decided to join my mother's cousin and his family and flee to Marseille by boat from Porto Santo Stefano. A dangerous move but one I knew was the only chance for my family."

Harry noticed how Leonardo emphasized and referred to the family as "his".

Chapter Thirty Five

Joe woke up to someone knocking on the store front door. Who the fuck is waking me up at six on my day off, he muttered to himself. He turned around and as in slow motion his right foot slipped into the left slipper followed by the left foot into the right slipper. It didn't matter because the slippers were so worn an elephant could fit in them. He walked across the room to the rusty hook on the wall where he kept his robe. The gray, dirty robe was too small and was hanging down like a blanket. Everything about Joe had seen its best days and he slowly moved down the stairs, still muttering to himself as if anyone really cared. He almost tripped over his own feet losing his right slipper which like an airplane with a broken wing flew down the stairs.

"Who the hell wants me so bad at six in the morning. Better be Sophia Loren or her fucking sister."

His robe, half open, revealed a big fat belly hiding what once may have been a man capable, but highly unlikely, of getting the attention of Sophia Loren.

About a week ago he had seen Maria and Harry leave for Italy and on this gray and rainy Monday morning he was wondering if they had located the family in the picture, thinking it may be Harry having returned to tell him about what he had found out. Joe hadn't paid any attention to it at all since they left. He just assumed Harry was going to get in touch with him once he found the family or the fate of them. Not hearing from him for over a week now made him think it was Harry waking him up.

The knocking became louder and frenzied and impatient. Knock, knock, knock in fast and loud succession.

"I'm on my way. It's only six on Monday morning." Joe, now screaming, losing his temper like he did so many times in the past. It was like the last thirty years of living peacefully in Cold Spring had been erased from his life and he was back to the gambling and mobster behavior he had lived on the west coast. And it had all began with the phone call from the asshole Frank asking him to locate the family in the picture.

"I'm coming, I'm coming," he once more screamed, now at the door, unlocking and opening it to give the piece of shit a lesson or two of manners he thought to himself.

His jaw dropped faster than the rest of his fat face managed to do, leaving him with a rather stupid look when there stood Frank on the other side of the door.

"Hey Joe, you little piece of shit. How long does it really take for you to bring your fat ass down here to open the door?" Frank swung the door open, pushed Joe away and entered into the store, almost tripping on a small wooden chair. With a well-placed kick for a man who wasn't much fitter than Joe, he sent the chair flying, landing next to the store counter, one leg braking off, flying over the counter and landing next to the cash register. A bodyguard followed him, closing the door behind them in a more gentle and quiet way.

"Oh, oh…Joe stammered out when being pushed back, almost falling over the chair. The store was small and like all antique stores had more things than what could fit onto the shelves or aisles. Customers, who mostly came up from the crowded New York City, expected it and wouldn't feel comfortable otherwise.

"Wha..a…t are you doing here..?" He continued to stammer and moved behind the counter. His three sizes too small robe almost fell off when he turned around the corner. He tripped again and to prevent him from falling grabbed on to the crank on the old fashioned cash register with both of his hands. The sound of rolling gears when he grabbed the machine, and then a kind of clunking alongside the ding when the slide of the drawer fully extended with a thud, was quickly drowned in a thunderous laughter by Frank.

Frank continued to laugh and said, "I'm not here to rob you. What possibly could you offer me anyway?" Frank laughed so hard he had to lean his left hand on the counter to prevent him from falling.

It was comic seeing the two of them, both fat, looking at least ten years older than their age, trying to desperately control their movements, one out of fear, the other because he was laughing so hard.

The bodyguard took a step forward to grab onto Frank who quickly pushed him away, throwing his arms up as if to say I'm ok, don't touch me.

"There you see, Joe, a kid who knows his place." referring to Lorenzo the bodyguard who now had positioned himself on a safe distance from both Frank and Joe, at the end of the counter to the right of the two fat men.

Joe was still holding on to the now open cash register when Frank turned to him and lashed out:

"Joe, you little piece of shit. Did you fucking get hold off the family I asked you to find or is that friend of yours with an attitude doing that for you as well? I mean, is there anything you CAN do?"

With a smirk on his face, the same one Joe had hated ever since he got involved with Frank to pay off his gambling debt and drug addiction, he was staring at Joe, waiting for an answer.

"My friend Harry is in Perugia, Italy and I'm just waiting for him to get back to me," Joe said and continued without thinking. "And his girlfriend, Maria, whose mother apparently had some connection with the family is with him."

"You better have a damn good reason for not telling me about this until now." Frank didn't exactly mean to be lenient about it although it fooled Joe who didn't think it was a big deal replying:

"Well, I was waiting to hear back from him about his findings. He left about a week ago and as of yet I haven't heard anything." Joe relaxing, losing his grip on the cash register, thinking Frank wasn't as upset about the whole thing after all.

"What the hell are you telling me?" Frank screamed out as if he wanted Harry to hear him all the way to Italy. "Why haven't you fucking called and threatened the guy and his girlfriend to come up with some information?" Frank looked like he was about to explode. "Are you freaking mad?

Joe grabbed on to the cash register again to control his urge to reach over the counter with his hands to strangle the son of a bitch who so consistently and deliberately made fun of him.

"What's the name of the family?" Frank yelled once more, spitting out the words that hit Joe in the face.

"Perugino, you son of a bitch." Joe screamed back. He'd had it with Frank.

With Frank turning around the counter to go after Joe for insulting him, Joe glanced over and noticed the old revolver in the open cash register, the same revolver he had put there that day when Harry had walked in on him. It was the revolver Frank had given to him to get rid of but never did.

He quickly grabbed it from the open cash register, aimed at the oncoming Frank but before any shot was fired a silent puff, puff came from Frank's side. Joe, still with the revolver in his hand and with big eyes, starred at Frank who took a step back when he heard the puff, puff from the silencer of his bodyguard's pistol. Joe's blood spewed like a volcano spitting out its lava from the open wound right around his left chest area. He didn't make a sound. He just stared at Frank. Blood poured from his mouth almost at the same furious pace as from the open wound in his chest. Joe slid silently down with a thump behind the counter.

Joe's life ended the same violent way he had lived it. Fate had turned up in the most ugly, terrible way possible in the shape and form of Frank, the man who had made Joe pay not only for his gambling debt by killing, but by the hands of the same corrupted, evil, violent and despicable human being he once called the boss.

"The little piece of shit was more stupid than I thought." Frank wiped off some blood that had splashed on his face, hands and clothing.

"Lorenzo, take the cash from the register, wipe off the counter where I was leaning and make it look like a robbery." With surgical precision, the bodyguard reacted to the situation swiftly and without emotions.

"I'll wait for you in the car. Make it look like someone tried to enter the front door with force before you leave."

Frank was still wiping off some blood when Lorenzo came back, started the car, drove up the deserted Main Street in Cold Spring and left the town without notice.

It was 6:20 that rainy and grey Monday morning when Joe finally paid off his debt to Frank...with his life.

"Get Alitalia on the line. We are not heading back to LA. We have some unfinished business to take care of in Italy first." Frank threw out the paper napkins with blood on them once they crossed Bear Mountain Bridge and told Lorenzo to buy two round trip tickets to an airport close to Perugia, flying out from Newark Liberty International Airport on the next available flight.

Chapter Thirty Six

"Once we arrived to Marseille we immediately got in touch with the French resistance. They took us to the professor. I told you he taught us enough English to keep us safe from the Germans."

Leonardo looked at Harry who nodded. No mention of his father, thought Harry, yet he knew the last about his fate had not been told.

"Very shortly after arriving, I found out that our contacts with the resistance were involved in the drug trafficking business." Leonardo continued. "It was easy money. Because of the war the demand was high. I needed the money to take care of my mother, sister and brother. I was the head of the family now."

Leonardo paused. It was the second time he had mentioned how important it was for him to act like the head of the family despite his young age at the time.

Harry looked up and saw Leonardo staring at the door just a few feet away from him. As if he expected someone to walk in. It was quiet. It had been this way since the joy and laughter had left the house when they all, in haste, had fled to Marseille in 1944, not to return.

A hero to his family, a villain to others and once a violent and criminal member of the drug cartels in New York, Leonardo had suffered in silence and had nothing to be ashamed of, or to regret, in his mind. He did what was necessary and he did it on his own, secretly and efficiently, keeping his family in the dark about his efforts. Until now.

The joy was gone. It had been for a while. Ever since growing up with an abusive father who they could all forget about, at least when he was at work. It was in those moments, and only in those moments, they were able to relax and laugh without fear of being the target of his anger.

Leonardo, when not working at the bakery, could enjoy a few moments of joy with his siblings, mother and, in brief moments of teenage love, with Maria's mom, his little brother's babysitter. He never forgot her and if he would have known she had moved to the US shortly after he left Marseille, he would have sought her out.

When Maria stood at his doorstep next to Harry the other day, he was once more reminded about a time, the only time, he had been in love. It was a teenage love, so pure, innocent and different from the life he had lived growing up in the same house he was living in with a big successful vineyard next to it. His criminal drug trafficking and secret life in Marseille and New York and his lonely but peaceful life back in Perugia since returning almost seventy years ago stood in sharp contrast to the feelings about a past stirred up by Maria showing up at his doorstep. Time had once more turned back in his mind and he was in a place he had been longing for ever since returning back in 1953. Now he could tell.

His side of life, torn between the love of his mother, sister and brother and the distain for his father. The circumstances that led him into a violent and criminal double life with secrets so difficult to bear, unable to share.

Until now.

In the distance the workers were chatting in Italian, their voices fading away as they were heading out to the fields. It turned silent again. Leonardo's face stern. His body stiff like a lion about to kill. As if he expected someone or something to happen. The dark eyes and the intense stare expressed hate and fury, thinking back to a time he'd rather not remember, yet wanting to desperately tell and reconcile with the world. To look back, not with anger but with joy and appreciation because he had kept the family together. And safe.

Leonardo said nothing for a long time. He looked down at the photograph Harry had given to him on the first day they met. His eyes brightened. His facial expressions less tense, and Harry could even see a soft smile when he gently moved his fingers over the picture. He lifted his hand, put two fingers on his lips, gave them a gentle kiss and placed the kiss on his mother in the picture.

Harry looked at the man behind the heavy oak desk. What he saw was a man of strength, dignity and power, a man with a lot of compassion for the things he cared for and loved. One who took advantage of the opportunities, but who wished he'd been able to make other choices.

At the young age of eighteen, he had started down a path few men ever travel. A choice so life changing that once he made it there was no turning back. Having to lie to his family to protect them and leaving them behind without a word of explanation, was like cutting short a life that, despite his length of life, in some ways had ended at age of eighteen.

"It all happened so quickly. The drugs were flowing in at a faster pace the closer we got to the end of the war. It was like Marseille wasn't part of the war. More like a free port with its own rules and business practices. So that's how I, through drugs, ended up in New York after the war, getting myself and my family a free ride to the promised land."

Leonardo sounded poetic. He looked up at Harry and took a moment to be sure Harry was taking notes.

"This is important, my friend. I had responsibilities now, and the war gave me a chance to make easy money in a war stricken and corrupt Marseille. Opportunities just presented themselves and I took advantage."

Harry looked up, glanced over at Leonardo who with an almost shameful expression, was close to an apology for the kind of business he had been involved in and that had supported his family for many years. Leonardo's face quickly turned serious again and with pain written all over it screamed:

"I hate my father for putting my family at risk."

"But he got what he deserved in the end…"
Leonardo relaxed again and smiled.

"I did to the piece of shit the one thing he never expected. I got back at him for all the violence, the beating of my mother, my little brother and me and treating his own daughter like a slave." An eye for an eye, is what we know and I ended the violence and deception by giving him a taste of his own medicine."

Harry anticipated it but still got the chills when Leonardo finally uttered the words:

"I killed the fucking bastard, and it was the best thing I´ve ever done for my family."

Chapter Thirty Seven

Harry stared down at his notes. He read the line he'd just written down over and over.

I killed the fucking bastard, and it was the best thing I´ve ever done for my family."

Somehow it didn't come as a surprise to him what Leonardo had just told him. What surprised him was the calm that followed after he angrily had revealed the secret he had carried for so long and with the vigor he had slammed his fist onto the oak desk.

Leonardo looked relieved. A heavy burden had just fallen off his shoulders. And a secret he had carried with him for well over seventy years without anyone knowing.

"You see, Harry," Leonardo picked up where he had left off staring at Harry with eyes black as a Scandinavian winter night. "My father was a Nazi collaborator and was not only going to turn in his own wife because she was a Jew, but perhaps us, the children because we were the products of a Jew. Or, he could take us kids up north to where the Germans were holding out while the allies were moving up from the south at a very rapid pace."

Harry, now bursting with curiosity of how Leonardo had killed his father and the aftermath. How nobody knew or had known all these years, what sparked his father to turn against his own family, wanting to turn in his own wife to the Germans and by bringing his kids to the Nazi controlled north, putting them in danger.

Harry wasn't going to wait for Leonardo to continue.

"Why? Why Leonardo?," He finally got the courage to ask.

"Harry, my friend," Leonardo asked in a rhetorical manner, "why do people do things we can't imagine anyone doing? Out of fear, he said answering his own question.

His words echoed in the room they had been sitting in for the last four days. It felt like his words filled up the whole house. A house with a history, and many unanswered secrets. Finally the whole story was told for the first time. Soon the words and his story were going to be all over the news. Harry knew this was going to be his big breakthrough. He caught himself thinking how odd it was to stumble onto this story after all these years of waiting.

Why do people do things we can't imagine anyone doing? It was like those words summarized the whole life of Leonardo. Yet, they boiled down to one single powerful word.

Fear.

What else brings a human being to the brink of doing things we can't imagine anyone doing. The fuel behind the breaking point is the fear of losing something or someone. Fear of not being enough, not being wanted, not being loved or appreciated. Or worse, fear of death or someone close to dying.

"On June 29, 1944, the small village of Civitella in Val di Chiana, was set on fire. All grown men massacred, women raped and children left to mourn by the Germans, who desperately retreated from their positions just west of us and north of Rome. The allies were quickly taking possession of southern Italy and in the wake of the Germans leaving for the still Nazi controlled north, they plundered, killed and raped every village in their path. The Germans acted out of fear…fear of being killed if not killing first…"

Harry, not aware of the fate of Civitella in Val di Chiana, realized the enormous pressure and fear under which the Perugino family lived. Those last couple of months and days, the Germans were literally in their backyard and the Allied forces stormed through their front yard. They were caught in the middle of it all. Scared, desperate and not knowing what was going to happen to them.

"Word spread quickly about the massacre in Civitella and the other villages close by. My father told me, and me only, about his plans to leave early morning of July 1st, two days after the massacre in Civitella. I knew he wasn't going to take my mom with us."

Leonardo looked over towards the door again. Did he expect anyone or did the door remind him about the escape plan and decision he made to save his mother from certain death and in the case of his siblings, a deportation to Germany or slaughter in concentration camps as well? He turned his head and looked at Harry, his eyes much warmer than before, his face an expression of pain rather than anger, his posture like the old man he was rather than the stoic younger man he portrayed.

"My friend," he said again to Harry, while leaning over the big oak desk with an unobstructed view of the door on which he fixated. Harry was sitting to Leonardo's left making notes about the fascinating story unraveling before him. A story he knew was going to be the most powerful he had ever written and one that would give him a tremendous boost and recognition at a rather late stage of his photo journalistic career.

"I'm only going to tell you this once so you better listen to what I'm about to tell you," Leonardo whispered with an emotional voice, almost cracking under the tension and feelings stirred up by reliving the dramatic days back in June and July of 1944.

Chapter Thirty Eight

"My father called me to a meeting in this same room on the eve of June 30' 1944. The same day we had received the word about the massacre in Civitella. He sat down behind the desk, in the very same chair I'm sitting in now."

Leonardo stroked the hard but worn oak surface.

"And then he just cold heartedly threw the news in my face. I remember it to this day...the exact words he used. He said: "We are Catholics, not Jews. We don't belong here. We belong with our comrades up north. Our allegiance is not with the Italians and certainly not with the Jews. We will have a future in the Third Reich. You, your brother, sister and me…""

"He then raised his right arm in support and with a loud, ice cold voice said Heil Hitler."

Leonardo sat quietly and stared at the door again.

"My father was heartless." Leonardo screamed out the words.

Harry felt the anger in the room and saw the rage on Leonardo's face. It was this incident and everything that followed over the next eight years that shaped him and turned him from a normal eighteen year old young adult to a fierce killer, drug dealer and mobster.

His father's words, actions and a complete disregard for the fate of his mother, was what made Leonardo grab the Lupara sawed-off shotgun laying right in front of him on the desk. He calmly aimed it at his father who with an open mouth as if trying to say something, stood up and took a few steps back. No words came out of his mouth.

He looked at his son in disbelief. The fear in his eyes said it all. He couldn't utter a single word even if he tried. He just stared at his son when the shots hit him fast and furious. The multiple wounds inflicted by the sawed off shotgun killed him instantly.

"I killed the bastard and it saved us all."

The calm that followed replaced the horrific way the echo of the words just spoken.

Leonardo kept on staring at the door. Again, Harry wondered why.

"You know Harry, this room was my father's and no one ever came in here. We kids had no idea what was in here. My father always kept it locked. It has a separate entrance." Leonardo looked over at the door again.

"Through this door, I now know, many Nazi supporters walked in and out from secret meetings my father hosted during the War."

"And through this door the body of my father was carried out to the fields nearby where I spent most of the night digging his grave."

Harry interjected for the first time.

"How were you able to keep it a secret from the rest of the family?"

Without acknowledging, not even looking over at Harry, Leonardo continued:

"My mother and siblings were over at her cousin's house that night and didn't return until the following morning to the news that my father had left us to travel north and had told me he wouldn't' return. You see, it wasn't like we didn't know he was a Nazi supporter. We just didn't think he was actually going to just leave but this was kind of not unexpected and the way he had treated us. Who really cared?"

Harry was just about to ask another question when Leonardo with a dismissive movement with his hand and an irritated look on his face continued:

"It was the morning of July first and our cousin had just told my mother and siblings that there was no time to lose. He had planned to travel to Marseille and asked if we wanted to come with him."

Harry had many questions, but knew he had to wait for Leonardo to allow him to ask.

"We just packed a few things, some clothes and personal items, and left the same evening to go back to my mother's cousin's home. The next day we were off to Marseille. Everything happened so fast we never got a chance to say goodbye to the rest of our family and friends.

"My father leaving us behind just made our decision so much easier. You know, Harry, no one really missed him. We were all very relieved."

"Me killing him was an act of mercy…it saved my mother from certain death and us from a likely death if he would have been allowed to go through with his plans to bring us up north. To the Germans."

Harry had a hard time with all the information being revealed at such a fast pace. It felt like he had gone through the life story of Leonardo in minutes rather than days.

What's next, Harry thought to himself.

"Well, in less than forty-eight hours after I killed and buried my father, we were in Marseille." Leonardo continued.

"I never got a chance to mourn or to grasp what I had done. It was so easy, so painless, so rewarding and so relieving to put the bullets in him. To see his look of disbelief. His scared look and for the first time not being in control. Instead he was being controlled by no other than his own son, firing bullets in him before he even knew what was happening. He didn't utter a word. His facial expression said it all right before he closed his eyes and no understanding. He died the same way he had lived.

Leonardo, now quite red in the face, anger in his voice, took a deep breath and looked over to the door again – the fourth time he had done so in minutes.

It was the very same door he had entered to see his father on that evening of June 30 over seventy years ago. The same door he had carried the body of his father through to bury him in the fields outside.

The same fields where now the vines were growing.

The same fields that made Leonardo a rather wealthy man.

"And then we arrived to Marseille. The war had saved me from my crazy sociopath of a father and certain death. But the war was also a curse. It forced me to turn into the criminal I became once I got involved in the French mob and the mobster families of New York."

Chapter Thirty Nine

Maria awakened. The wind had picked up and the window shutters slammed against the frame in sync with the nearby church bell. Maria counted the number of strikes and when it stopped at ten she threw the sheet aside, stood up and stretched her naked, fit and beautiful body while strolling over to the window to close it.

Maria was in love. More importantly, the feelings even when he wasn't physically present but only in her mind, were nothing more than euphoric.

She quickly jumped into the shower. Today was an important day. She was going to meet the rest of her extended family who were gathered at her Aunt's farm right outside Perugia. Harry, who was now at Leonardo's vineyard for the fourth day, was going to join her in the evening at the farm for a big and traditional Italian dinner feast. She was so looking forward to the day and evening, grateful to Leonardo for helping her find her family and for Harry to share it with her.

The day was going to be beautiful and the evening even better she thought to herself. Grabbing her purse on the fly, rushed outside and turned around the corner to the always waiting line of taxis.

She gave the driver the address. Her thoughts were with Harry and she wondered how he was doing. If it wasn't for the meeting with her family she would have joined him. It was a good thing she didn't. Their journey was going to take a dramatic turn and they were going to find themselves on the plane back home earlier than expected.

Chapter Forty

Harry was listening to Leonardo's fascinating story about the years in New York after he and his family arrived on July 17, 1945, and his leaving in 1953, never to return, nor see his family ever again.

It was only a couple of weeks after they arrived in the US that he had located and gotten involved with the mobsters he had been told to contact by the French mob. Soon the flow of narcotics into New York increased at a rate of speed and in never before seen quantities. However never enough it seemed to satisfy the demands for the drugs. After the war the use of narcotics sky rocketed and mobster families quickly adjusted their business from liquor to heroin and opium.

With the money Leonardo made, he was able to help support his family and get his mother up and running in a legit business, importing the same Perugina brand chocolate she and her husband had been producing over the years back in Perugia. The connections she had turned out to be very useful, and after the war the business went from being solely an Italian product to become a worldwide known quality chocolate.

Mrs. Perugino set up her confectionary store on Arthur Avenue in the Bronx, a neighborhood with a large Italian heritage and the closest she could come to feel like she was back in Italy. Italian was spoken all the day long and the families in the neighborhood knew each other by first names.

When the war was over, Mrs. Perugino soon became associated with the Perugina brand and the Baci kisses up on Arthur Avenue and soon the whole city of New York knew of her.

Leonardo and his mobster friends used her business as a cover and money laundering for their illegal drug profits. This was something he earlier in the day had told Harry was the least proud moment of his past in the US. Thankfully, by the time he left in 1953, his mother had turned her business into a very successful enterprise on its own merits and the mob stopped using the store as a cover. Instead other, less successful businesses were being used. Her first store on Arthur Avenue and the stores that followed on the Upper East side, had become too much of a news item. With the New York Times, The New Yorker and some national magazines and papers writing stories about her successful enterprise, she became a celebrity, and a success story for immigrants coming over at the end of the war. The mob didn't mind publicity but this was too close and with too much attention for comfort. Instead they found other stores and businesses to use as their cover for the ever increasing drug trafficking.

When Leonardo left in 1953, he had been promised by the crime syndicate that his family was going to be protected and left alone. Leonardo had done his job, paid his dues but the benefits were not for him to enjoy.

His family never had to look over their shoulders like he had to every day of the week and all hours of the day and night. They were completely unaware of the business that had supported them in the beginning, and in shock when Leonardo one day simply disappeared. That day was the same date they had sailed into the New York harbor, eight years earlier.

Leonardo's eyes steadfast staring at the door thinking back to that day in July 1953 when everything he had built was taken away from him. One day he was the King and had everything. A good life in America, friends and family. Now faced with a sudden departure for the second time in his life he knew he had to tell everything to Harry. It was much tougher to tell this secret. Again, he protected his family and the family's honor. His love for his mother, brother and sister, the business he had developed and the huge success of the chocolatier business his mother had started were all there for him to reap the benefits from.

It was the murder of someone that forced him to leave. It was something he did for his family. Eight years to the day, after arriving, he left and went back to Perugia for the last time, to stay there for the rest of his life. No return and no contact with his family. It was a very high price to have to pay to fire those bullets into that man's crotch. To see him suffer before finishing him with two more bullets into his head, blowing his brains all over the sofa.

Chapter Forty One

The taxi driver stopped in front of a beautiful garden just a short ride outside Perugia. The niece of Francesca, Maria's mom, came almost sprinting down the short walk from the small brick building she had lived in all her life with her mother, Francesca's sister Angelica. Sophia, a couple of years younger was just like Maria. Fit, full of energy and beautiful. When Maria first met her four days ago, she immediately saw a resemblance to her own mother in her, with her straight nose, warm and hazel eyes and ebony black hair she was seemingly a picture of perfection.

Sophia's smile, almost an exact copy of Francesca's, warmed up the cool morning and brightened up the world around her, like the sun rising over the Apennine mountain ridge right behind her. Just like Maria remembered her mom's smile waking up in the early cool Fall mornings back in Cold Spring, to get ready for school. The warm smile she delivered each and every time she gently kissed her goodbye, seeing her off at school before heading over to open up the café. This gave Maria the confidence and strength she would need throughout her life, especially during the tough years with Robert. His drug abuse and alcoholism had almost ruined her teenage daughter's lives before Maria stood up for herself and them, using all her positive reinforcement she had been taught as a child growing up in Cold Spring with her single parent mom.

Wearing a simple white dress with a gold color braided belt, her hair long, wavy sienna brown and her blue eyes shining, She greeted Sophia who, with open arms and a kiss on each cheek clutched Maria when she stepped out from the taxi.

"You look gorgeous." Sophia exclaimed.

With her arms around Maria's waist she looked at her with tears of joy falling down her beautiful cheek bones.

"Maria, you are the sister I never had. I am so very happy you came to visit us. Let's make sure we never lose sight of each other ever again."

They turned around and arm in arm started to walk down the short path to Sophia's house. It was a beautiful morning and the two of them were stunningly gorgeous, like a painting of two goddesses brought to life. Their eyes sparkling like stars flaunted on the night sky, while the morning sun cast a warm, bright light on them.

Maria turned to Sophia and placed a gentle, friendly kiss on her cheek, smiled and was about to ask Sophia how come she never married, when the door opened and Sophia's seventy five year old mother Angelica, Maria's Aunt, greeted them with obvious joy that would have the world sigh with contentment.

The welcoming of a relative from far away and one who had made an effort to trace down her roots, was typical of an Italian family. The welcoming warmth when someone came to visit and the family got a reason to cook, uncork the wine, eat and drink for hours with not a single quite moment because everyone seemed to have something to say or ask of everyone else. Wine glasses were never empty and plates with food just kept coming and coming to the table. It was an endless stream of sharing their and the family's way of saying welcome to our home.

Today though was the perfect day for a reunion and introduction of Maria's new love later in the evening. Nothing could possibly go wrong.

"So fantastico to have you here, Maria," Angelica said smiling as bright as the sun rising to its highest point on the blue sky on what seemed to be a picture perfect day for a reunion with Maria as the guest of honor and with the introduction of Harry who were on the minds of many who couldn't wait to meet Maria's new love interest. Today their long lost relative from the States was visiting and a feast to welcome her and her lover was in full swing.

"I can't wait," Maria with a happy smile on her face screamed out for the whole world to hear. "Is there anything I can help you with?" turning to Angelica who quickly threw her an apron and replied:

"Of course. And while we cook we'll talk about you and everything that happened to your mom after she left with her American soldier. We want to know everything about Harry as well my dear Maria." she continued with a wink.

Maria was looking forward to this evening with excitement and pride, getting a chance to get know her Italian family and their friends and to introduce Harry to all of them. She couldn't wait.

"I'd love to help out," Maria turned around and went straight into the kitchen to start preparing the feast that would end up being her last night in Italy even though she and Harry weren't supposed to leave for another three days.

Chapter Forty Two

"Leonardo?"

Harry leaned over to catch a glimpse of Leonardo who had turned his face away from him to hide the tears in his eyes. A long silence had followed Leonardo's emotional story of leaving Perugia for Marseille, arriving to New York and the successful eight years he lived there with his mother, sister and little brother. They had, with a combination of their own hard work and success and Leonardo's connections with the New York City mob, found the American Dream. It had given them a start in the new country that had exceeded any expectations they had when arriving on July 17, 1945 to a place they knew very little about. At least they had some family members already living here who'd helped them out in the very beginning and made the transition a much smoother one than in Marseille.

The one year they spent there had been tough on them. Although hiding from the Nazis in the beginning, Marseille was liberated on August 27, 1944, only six weeks after their arrival and life slowly began to get back to normal. They probably would have decided to leave for the United States earlier if it had not been for Leonardo's involvement with the French mob, which was closely connected with the partisans.

The time in Marseille was tough on his sister and little brother. Leonardo took big risks working with the mob and now as the head of the Perugino family he made sure they stayed at a safe distance from his business dealings with the French.

It had left the rest of the family in isolation and fear of unseen enemies. They didn't know who to trust from day to day but also not knowing from a day to another what was happening with Leonardo. Would he return to them in the evening or not? They were constantly worried and had very little time to relax until they arrived in New York a year after arriving to Marseille. Now reunited with some old family members who had left Italy long before the war, life was much easier even if the work they put in was more than they ever had done before. Leonardo, busy day and night with his drug dealings, his mother with setting up her confectionary business and his sister and brother trying to keep up with their school work in a language they barely knew.

Leonardo slowly turned around, his eyes tearful. He, for the first time, looked his age.

"Yes Harry, where was I?"

Telling about his life up to this point seemed to have giving him a boost and with pride in his voice he had told the story about how he saved his family from certain death. Now though the story took another turn in that he was forced to face the reasons for his actions and all the secrets he had carried with him ever since that day when they were to celebrate their eight year anniversary of arriving to the States.

On the eve of July 17, 1953, Leonardo's life turned upside down. On that day he left the States, disappeared, never to return again or to see his family. The people he loved, the family he had killed for, supported and kept away from danger with his criminal activities were now safe.

"You see, my friend," Leonardo said as he stared at Harry with that still powerful, stern and cold look that he had stared down so many in the past, before threatening to kill them if they didn't do what he ordered. These were no empty threats. Though young, the innocence was long gone when he created the fear in the eyes of his enemy to get what he wanted. Anyone stupid enough to stand in his way by not doing what he told them to do, quickly found themselves digging their own graves with no chance of surviving despite their desperate pleas for lenience.

Leonardo was not about to show any.

"You see," he repeated more firmly, "It's been a long time but the days I spent in New York were the best and most productive of my life until the last day which is still painfully clear in my mind."

Harry expected another dramatic moment in Leonardo's life considering what the old man had told him. He knew something bad must have happened for Leonardo to leave the best days of his life behind, so suddenly and so secretly. Having to cut the ties with his family that he loved over everything else was a major issue.

227

For the next two hours Harry was transferred back in time, shadowing Leonardo on his last full day in the US before having to leave everything behind he had built along with his family. His illegal activities and drug trafficking, his mother a successful legitimate business and his sister and little brother on the verge of becoming US citizens, attending schools and getting an education Leonardo was never offered, nor had any interest in schooling. He had already gotten the taste for easy, and big money.

Chapter Forty Three

It was a day like the one exactly eight years ago when the Perugino family arrived on Ellis Island, the entry to the promised land. The temperature was a balmy 90 degrees with the usual July humidity you couldn't escape, even if you spent the whole day at the beach.

"Are you ready?" Leonardo whispered in his mother Rachel's ear when strolling up the long walkway to the mansion of his boss, Don Gagliano, head of the Lucchese crime family. Today was a day to remember for the whole Perugino family so Rachel, Angelina, Eduardo and Leonardo were all invited to the annual summer party to celebrate the success of Leonardo, making his fortune in the "import business" as Leonardo always referred to it when his mother asked "What is his business again?" But they were also celebrating the day exactly eight years ago when they first arrived to the US.

Eduardo, now seventeen, was a high achieving student. Earlier in May, he graduated with honors from High School and was now destined for Fordham University in the fall. Rachel made sure some of their fortune building a successful Perugina chocolate business had been put aside for Eduardo's further education.

Then of course there was the very pretty Angelina, now twenty, attending her junior year at Cornell University with a PHD degree in psychotherapy in sight. Azure blue, dreamy eyes, perfectly matching her black hair and slender body. Leonardo had always thought his family could be a picture perfect cover on a movie magazine. Few could argue that he was wrong. Of course with the exception of his father they may have qualified as the picture perfect "familia."

His and Eduardo's genes obviously were very much like their father, but how Angelina ended up with Mediterranean azure blue eyes always had been a topic for some suspicions that Franco wasn't the father. There obviously had been many years in Rachel's and Franco's marriage when they had lived apart. Franco on one hand depressed and finding his life dominated by his political views and allegiance to "il fascismo" and later the Nazis. Rachel worked hard but always seemed to find time for her children as often and as much as possible.

"Wait for us." said Angelina with a soft voice matching her grace and innocence.

"Of course little sister," Leonardo turned his head and with a broad smile he exclusively saved for family members, and especially for his sister to who he'd always been very close. He waited for her and Eduardo to catch up. Together they entered the mansion and were greeted with cheers and looks of appreciation among the many guests, some of them movie stars and artists themselves. The Lucchese crime organization had strong ties with the entertainment industry along the East Coast.

Soon after arriving Leonardo excused himself to greet the host, Don Gagliano. Rachel was busy chatting with the society ladies of upper Manhattan and Long

Island, making sure to remind them to come and visit her confectionary stores. Eduardo quickly ran over to the beautiful younger daughter of Don Gagliano, who was happy to see him. They both had met at parties on Long Island while in High School.

Angelina, now surprisingly finding herself left alone, began moving across the large room in a confident manner, grabbing a champagne glass from one of the many waiters passing by, and without turning noticed all the encouraging looks from the young men standing by the open bar across the room.

Angelina certainly had many opportunities over the last couple of years to find a rich and successful boyfriend of Italian descent, like the ones represented at today's party. But, Angelina wasn't like her friends her age. She was determined to do something with her life. To get an education and to make sure she would be independent from a man like Leonardo, her brother, who she continued to adore.

Not a man who looked at her only with admiration and desire for her beauty alone. Rather a man who shared an interest in the intelligent young woman she was and the strong person she had become growing up. Getting a chance to attend college was a great opportunity to build her own future, without being dependent on a stylish rich Italian like the ones she saw plenty of around the room. Did she enjoy the attention? Of course. But of greater importance she wanted a man who could see deeper and find the sensitive and intelligent woman she had become.

She always drew attention. As she read through a section of text in one of her books at college, the highlighted section stood out, tuning out sensations and perceptions that are not relevant at the moment. She instead focused her energy on the information.

She was hoping that one day someone would see her as the highlighted section of the room, of his life, beyond the beauty she radiated on the surface. To look deeper into an intelligent woman with a sensitive mind. This was a woman with a determination to do what was right and what was in the best interest of not only her, but the wellbeing of others.

The men across the room stared at her with desire and attraction. She found their looks degrading. The strong person she had become growing up with her mother as a role model was the precise intelligence the men gathered today despised. Or rather they had no clue how to handle a woman who spoke her own mind, being as strong on her own as she would be for the man she would fall in love with and the family they one day would create.

No, these men were celebrating a life that had but one goal. To maximize their own wealth and have a wife to stay home and raise their children.

Despite her own good fortune to have and live a comfortable life and getting to go to college for a degree many of her friends couldn't or wouldn't have the courage to ask for, she never had or would take it for granted. She had lived a poor life in Italy growing up. A sheltered life in hiding in Marseille and arrived to a new country, new language and culture at the age of twelve without anything more than the clothes she was wearing and a small trunk filled with personal items. She and her family had made their fortune from nothing more than desire and a strong work ethic.

But, she knew.

She knew that Leonardo's successful "import" business wasn't entirely a "clean" operation. She had never said anything to her mother or to Leonardo. Their respective successes being unrelated to each other. Her mother building a chain of Perugina chocolate stores by herself, determined to succeed in the new country. Her brother who she had so much appreciation and love for, who had saved them many times after their father disappeared without a trace on the eve of their escape to Marseille.

Her one concern was Eduardo who looked up to his big brother Leonardo as the hero of the family; successful, handsome and respected. From a teenage High School honor student's viewpoint, he had the ultimate lifestyle. Freedom, with no teachers or professors, telling him what to do, think or be. The bright future waiting for him after attending Fordham prep school and now enrolled at Fordham University to complete his major in Finance was unlimited. This though was all threatened by his desire to be like Leonardo, Angelina believed.

"Miss Perugino," a voice right behind her whispered in her ear and awakened her from her thoughts about why she was here today, surrounded by men and women she didn't have much in common with. Turning around she was looking at Giulio, a handsome Italian in his mid-thirties who she believed, after seeing him at other parties in the past with their host, Don Gagliano, was close to the family.

"Oh, I'm sorry Miss. I didn't mean to startle you," he slurred having had a drink or two too many. He wasn't drunk but had just enough to fit into the picture Angelina had drawn about most of the attending guests. But a handsome Italian, Angelina caught herself thinking, and likely an important connection for Leonardo, she decided to stay around and chat.

"Hello I'm Angelina," she introduced herself knowing very well it wasn't customary for her to take the initiative. But she wasn't about to change because she was at a party with Leonardo's business partners and friends.

"I'm Giulio, and I know who you are," he quickly replied with just enough arrogance to annoy Angelina. She took a step back to avoid Giulio's clumsy move to lean forward, attempting to steal a kiss. The whiskey he was holding in his hand spilled over, just missing Angelina's beautiful white dress. She turned around and walked away. Giulio dismissed the waiters who quickly had come to his help, regained his balance and strolled over to the bar, where some of the men greeted him while others quickly left the bar area.

Rachel who had seen the incident from her position chatting with the women across the room, excused herself and went after Angelina who had walked outside to the perfectly manicured garden; a venetian masterpiece that had made it to the cover page of Life Magazine last month. Rachel, while looking around trying to locate Angelina, was thinking who the guy was that had spoken to Angelina. She too recognized him but since she wasn't very familiar with Leonardo's business and friends she didn't know him.

Rachel wasn't going to see Angelina until later that evening when Leonardo brought her back home. It was the last time Rachel would see her son Leonardo.

Chapter Forty Four

Angelina had found a peaceful spot in a secluded corner of the garden, on a bench away from the noise. Here she could hide from the people she wanted to escape from and had no interest in meeting. The men her brother Leonardo was working with. Men with cynical views. She never could put her finger on what the "tailor made Italians" in their expensive suits were up to. They were successful businessmen just like Leonardo. Successful but arrogant.

During her studies at Cornell to become a psychotherapist, Angelina was much more interested in the attitudes and behavior of these people she met through Leonardo, than forming any friendships nor attachments.

Then her life turned upside down. Without any opportunity to think, the peace was shattered.

She never heard him coming.

She didn't know how. She didn't know why. She never got a chance to say anything, or scream. She was silenced by fear. The kind of fear that paralyzes thought. There was nothing she could do but to wish it would stop…that he would stop.

She knew then that her innocence was gone.

Lost forever.

She knew why she never liked the people around Leonardo. And she knew why she would hate them for the rest of her life.

The hand over her mouth. The whispering from behind, the cowardly approach of a man who had no decency, who forced himself on everything he wanted without any concern for anyone's feelings but his own. The voice telling her to keep quiet if she didn't want the knife he casually waived in front of her beautiful face to cut deep into her cheek, permanently scaring her face and lips.

He continued to whisper his threats in her ear as he slowly removed his hand from her mouth, holding the sharp edge of the knife so close to her cheek bone she could feel it inside her, as if he already had cut her open.

Angelina couldn't move; couldn't scream; couldn't feel. She was overcome by fear. But when the hateful character moved his hand from her mouth to under her dress, up her thigh and with a violent move ripped her underwear, she did feel.

She felt disgust and hatred unknown to her previously.

His hand on her thigh, felt cold and hard, like a heavy rock falling on top of her body. Paralyzed by the feel of the knife and his steadfast grip on it, with any sudden move would slice open her face, he, with his other hand started to unbuckle his belt and pull his pants down. With his body pushing her to the ground, she could do nothing to prevent this lowlife from forcing himself on her. The spineless coward, using violence on a defenseless woman, threatening to kill her if she didn't do what he asked of her, didn't stop.

She felt nothing when he forced himself inside her. The pain came later, and stayed with her for the rest of her life. Instead of the screams she dared not utter, the fear and anger turned to tears streaming down her cheeks and onto the blade of the knife. She was thinking about Perugia, her childhood, and Leonardo protecting her from her father's rage. She was thinking how much she wished to be back there feeling safe again. With Leonardo, her big brother, always being there for her.

When Leonardo found his sister sometime later, she kept on repeating the name "Giulio" and the words; "please take me home…to Perugia."

Chapter Forty Five

Harry looked up at Leonardo who had stopped talking. His eyes half closed, leaning over the desk, using both his arms to rest his tired and emotionally drained body. The rape of his sister wasn't only a tragedy for Angelina but a direct hit on his whole family. Once more he found himself in a position where he needed to act, swiftly and powerfully, whatever the consequences would be to protect them.

This beautiful but very tragic day turned out to be his last of many eventful days spent with the mob spanning back to Marseille in 1944, and the build-up of their drug cartel after the end of the war, up until now, eight years later.

"He got what he deserved." Leonardo screamed out, straightening his body, slamming both fists on the heavy oak desk surface. He now looked and acted more like the Leonardo Harry had gotten to know at the beginning of his arrival in Perugia. Strong, tough, vicious to his enemies and anyone who threatened him or his family. They were the only ones he showed compassion and empathy for.

"The son of a bitch violated my sister. It was a pleasure spreading the bastards brain all over the sofa that morning," he continued with an icy stare at Harry who shivered at the thought of having a gun pointed at him, waiting for the shot to go off, knowing what was coming.

The pain was for Leonardo and Angelina to feel. For the rest of their lives they would forever remember with sorrow the anniversary party in celebration of the family's arrival to New York eight years earlier.

Not talking about it was a secret they both maintained until now. Leonardo by agreeing to talk to Harry, decided it was time for someone to hear the story about their agony and pain but also success. The decision to kill his own father to protect and free the family from his insane decision to bring his kids to northern Italy and the Nazis, leaving their mother behind, was one that in the end made all this happen. The decisions Leonardo had made were courageous, dangerous and bold. What had happened to Angelina that evening was tragic and another devastating chapter in a dramatic, violent and criminal life. A life Leonardo had chosen so that he might be able to protect those he loved the most – his family.

*

After Leonardo had found Angelina he took her to one of the bedrooms upstairs in the mansion as Don Gagliano had insisted he do. Being very aware of the gravity of the situation and the implications that could follow. Any scandal or publicity could be devastating to his operation. He made sure Leonardo got all the help he needed to take care of his sister.

Don Gagliano's own doctor, who always was at his side during an event like this, had been called up to the room immediately. Before Angelina and Leonardo left later in the evening, Don Gagliano had made sure she was treated and that she would only see the physicians he decided were the best for her. Leonardo made Angelina understand the importance of seeing only them and no one else and not to discuss the rape with anyone, not even with their mother.

"I know Angelina, it's a lot to ask of you," Leonardo empathically told her. "But trust me, it's what's best for you, me and the rest of the family."

Angelina understood and she knew just too well what was at stake for Leonardo. In the criminal world he lived, one that Angelina never would accept or acknowledge existed, these things were not talked about. They were dealt with quietly. By people who could be trusted never to talk. Ever.

When she finally arrived back home with Leonardo, Rachel was waiting up for her, worried and wondering what had happened. She was relieved to hear she had gotten back to the mansion right after Rachel and Eduardo had left and that the only thing that had happened was that she got lost when strolling along the beach in the sunset hours.

*

Leonardo stopped. He stood up. Walked over to the window.

"I thought I heard a car", he said, then turned around to walk back to his chair. He sat down behind the oak desk that had been through so much over the years, just like the man now sitting behind it had.

Harry had heard the car as well but thought nothing about it. It's a car or a truck belonging to one the workers he thought to himself. He was wondering why Leonardo seemed concerned over a car approaching and why over the last couple of days had glanced over to the door, as if he expected a visitor. He guessed living a life like Leonardo had, you are bound to have a few enemies, even after all these years. It certainly seemed like Leonardo was on guard even after leaving the criminal and violent life behind in New York so many years ago.

The car that approached was, unknowingly, a reminder of a past Leonardo was afraid may catch up with him sooner or later. Little did he know of the surprise that would follow and the violence to which he once more had to revert. But for now he picked up the story again, turning to Harry who grabbed his pen, pressed the tape recorder play button and started to write.

Chapter Forty Six

Leonardo left Angelina with her mother and said:

"I just need to go back to Don Gagliano to wrap up a few things. I'll be back in the morning."

When he arrived back on Long Island it was already two in the morning and most of the guests had left. Leonardo met with Don Gagliano in his office on the first floor.

"Sorry Leonardo," he started off by saying before Leonardo interrupted him.

"Not your fault, Don." Leonardo wasn't looking for pity. He was looking for revenge.

"I know Giulio is your soldato." Leonardo was referring to his position as a made man in the Don's organization and one of the possible successors to the Don. "but you also know what he did to my sister and what my family means to me." He continued with anger and hostility in his voice that made Don Gagliano raise his hand with the hope of calming him down.

"I know, Leonardo…"

"So then Don you know what I have to do and what I'm asking for your permission to do," Leonardo continued calming down only slightly.

"I know." Don Gagliano repeated.

Leonardo waited silently but impatiently for the Don to say something.

"You know Leonardo how much I appreciate all you have done for me and my family," he after a long pause said. "You also know how much Giulio has meant to me. He's like the son I never had and was destined to take over one day."

Leonardo noticed the word "was" Don had used when describing his close relationship with Giulio.

"This is not easy for me," he continued looking up at Leonardo with a voice that, if translated into one word would have come out as "please". It was like, even though HE was the boss, was asking Leonardo to reconsider.

"I know that too, Don. Just too well," Leonardo replied thinking back to him killing his father in Perugia. An act of survival. A mindful killing. A mindful death. The same act of survival he now faced to honor his family and to seek revenge against the man who cowardly had violated a young innocent girl.

"But this is my sister we are talking about and…"

Don Gagliano again raised his hand to silence Leonardo.

"I hear you…" he quietly said and continued, "but it comes with a condition."

Leonardo wasn't prepared for this.

"You have my permission to take care of the problem but you need to promise me to leave right away,

244

never to return back to the US…ever. Do you understand?"

Leonardo didn't know what to think at first. Did he ask me to leave my family, my new country?

For what?

And to where?

As if the Don was reading his mind he continued:

"I need you to leave and go back to Italy, to Perugia where you are from and to stay there. I'll give you the money to start up a vineyard, get a new life and a new future. You are young. Find yourself a woman and have lots of bambinos."

Don Gagliano smiled. Leonardo didn't say anything. Just looked at the Don as if to beg him to reconsider. Something he would never ask because he knew this was the only option this powerful man would give him.

"I promise you we will take care of your family and give them everything they need. But by the looks of it your mother seems to have started a spectacular and profitable business all on her own so I don't know how much help they actually need." He continued to smile as if he found the whole situation amusing.

"You need to promise me that if they do need anything you would honor your word and not let them know where the help is coming from. And you can't tell them why and where I disappeared to."

"Don't worry Leonardo. It was never my intention to reveal the source of any help and certainly not what happened to you. That's part of the deal I'm offering. You would simply disappear and no one would ever know."

Leonardo just nodded, left the room and went upstairs where they had left Giulio. Not a word was spoken. Giulio was too drunk to even recognize Leonardo. The first shot hit right where his testicles had been before the impact. He felt every bit of the pain of them being blown into pieces. The pain sobered him up and he was looking at Leonardo with a stupid look of why. As if he didn't know what he had done and to whom. As if he thought he could get away with anything just because he was a made man.

He was too stupid to realize that when the second shot hit him right above where his balls once were that he had nowhere to go, that he was a marked man and was going to die on that sofa, that night. The last round blew his skull apart, scattering the pieces all over the white sofa.

Leonardo turned around and left the villa to ride to the airport, never to return.

Chapter Forty Seven

People were already seated by the time Harry arrived at the big welcoming party for Maria. He could hear the loud laughter, voices and music from a couple of blocks away. When entering the garden he saw Maria sitting at the head of a long table filled with the aroma of an Italian kitchen and the wonderful smell of many bottles of red wine, all uncorked and ready for consumption.

As if a whistle would have blown for halftime, everyone stopped what they were doing and looked up to see Harry entering the garden. The cheering and loud voices just multiplied.

"Ah, signore Harry, so great to finally meet you" one of the men closest to him said, stood up and gave him a strong but friendly hug.

On his way over to Maria, Harry had to stop at every seat. They all wanted to greet him with hugs and kisses. Maria, patiently waiting for him to work his way down the row, beamed with pride as she watched her Italian relatives and friends give Harry such a warm welcome.

When he finally reached the end of the table Maria was waiting for him with kisses reserved for the man she loved. Maria wrapped her arms around Harry and the cheers reached a crescendo. If it wasn't that they were sitting outside in the beautiful garden with the sun beaming down from a clear blue sky, the roof would have lifted. The whole village must have heard them. Harry smiled wondering if, as a matter of fact, everyone from the village was here already, gathered to greet their returning American relative.

"Come and sit down here next to me," Maria said after letting Harry loose.

Harry was happy to oblige, leaned over and whispered, "I love you," followed by "but we need to leave Italy tomorrow."

Maria first smiled, then looked at Harry with a curious and worried look.

"Is everything ok?" she asked.

"We are fine, nothing to worry about. We just need to leave a couple of days early. I need to get the article to print. My agent told me it was a rush."

He lied.

"But, Maria my love, tonight we'll celebrate your wonderful heritage and Italian family. What a feast they have arranged," Harry said convincingly although his thoughts were with Leonardo and what he believed must have happened back at the vineyard when the man entered through the door, the same door Leonardo so often had glanced at, during the last couple of day's conversations.

"Yes," Maria replied. "It doesn't matter we have to leave a couple of days early. What better way of ending our stay here in Perugia than having this fantastic party thrown in our honor," she screamed out for Harry to hear her over the crowd that had resumed their intense discussions, singing and laughing.

Harry had already changed the tickets on his way over to the party, knowing what he assumed had happened after he left Leonardo. There was no time to lose in getting out of Italy, for the safety of them both. Maria, with her possible ties to the Perugino family, although far back through her mother, was unaware of the potential danger of being associated with a former mobster, even if it went back seventy years.

Chapter Forty Eight

The car had stopped. Frank told his bodyguard to stay in the car. They had arrived in Perugia the same day and had no problem finding the vineyard of Leonardo who they had been told seldom left the farm. Once there, one of the workers had pointed to the house.

The door swung open and Frank entered. He just stood there, staring at Leonardo. Leonardo was the first to speak:

"Excuse me signor, how can I help you? If you like to buy some wine you should go to big house by the entrance to the vineyard. Georgina can help you and have you taste some of our best wines."

"I didn't come here to buy wine," Frank replied, glancing over to Harry and continued "You must be Harry. It's a pleasure to meet you. When I saw Joe the other day he kind of sent his regards, wishing you were back," Frank said first smiling, then adding a strange laugh, making the situation even more awkward than it already was.

Leonardo and Harry didn't see the humor in it. While sitting behind the oak desk facing Frank only a few feet away, Leonardo looked at Harry with surprise:

"Do you know him, Harry?"

"No can't say I do, only know about him," Harry replied realizing the man in front of them was Frank.

Why is he here? How did he know how to find Leonardo? He hadn't been in touch with Joe since arriving to Perugia, in part because he hadn't thought about it and part because the story he'd heard from Leonardo and its ties to Maria's past, had convinced him this was a story for him to hear and make public, and he alone. Sitting here facing Frank, who for reasons unknown, had traveled far to locate Leonardo, made Harry very uncomfortable.

Leonardo, noticing Harry's unease, knew immediately this wasn't a social call.

"So what's your name and why are you here if not to buy fine wine?" Leonardo stared at Frank with his cold, dark eyes leaving no doubt about how he felt having this man standing in front of him right where so many men before him had stood facing Leonardo's father. The secret meetings during the war, the plans to join the Germans, and Leonardo killing his father that evening in 1944, the day before Leonardo brought his family to safety in Marseille.

"I'm Frank, that's the only thing you need to know. Who I am have obviously not been of any interest to you for over seventy years so why now? What you really need to know is that I'm here to claim what's mine."

Leonardo's face showed no emotion, nor fear, staring down Frank with the same expression that Harry had seen many times over the last week listening to the exciting, while at the same time violent and scary, life story.

Was there a final twist to the life of Leonardo that Harry was about to witness?

Harry suspected that Frank's reason for revenge on the Perugino family went all the way back to Leonardo's criminal past in New York. But why wait so long to try and locate the family? Why seventy years? His name had never turned up during the week and obviously Leonardo didn't know him, or at least didn't recognize him.

That it was Frank, a mobster from the west coast who, through Joe, had asked Harry to locate the family in the picture, made it clear that this was now a dangerous situation. But, because of Maria's involvement and ties to the Perugino family, the story of Leonardo and his family had taken on a life on its own when Harry and Maria had arrived. Harry had brushed off the danger until now when Frank suddenly, in person, had appeared right in front of them. This was personal. And Frank was here to settle the score on an old mobster deal gone wrong. Seventy years in making.

Harry believed this must be Frank's intent and reason to travel all this way to personally confront Leonardo.

What now followed no one ever could have expected.

"You are looking at your son," Frank said, staring down Leonardo with a fierce look of anger and disgust.

It was Leonardo who spoke first.

"And how can I possibly have a son?"

"The same way all fathers get sons. By fucking mothers like my mother."

Harry looked over at Leonardo, his face tense and fists tightened. With a strong move he banged both his fists on the table that had seen so much, felt so much pain and violence over time. Leonardo just as quickly relaxed, leaned back in the chair, his arms down, resting comfortably on his legs. His whole body took a deep breath after the outburst and tense moment that followed.

Leonardo looked over at Harry in a deliberate move to avoid the gaze of the man standing in front of him, claiming he was his son.

"Harry, how do you know this man?"

Looking at Harry, waiting for his reply and not paying attention, he heard Frank repeat "I'm your son, and that's all you need to know."

"I only know him," Harry replied, glancing over at Frank, "by name and because he had the same picture of you and your family that Maria had. You know, the picture Maria gave you the first day we met."

"How does he know where I live? Did you tell him where to find me?" he continued with growing anger, avoiding Frank as if to not acknowledge his presence at all.

"No, no. I got the picture from a friend of mine back in the States and he apparently knew Frank. Then Maria of course found the same photograph as you already know and the fate of your family became of interest for not only Frank, who claims to be your son, but for Maria, when her mothers' relationship with you and your family became known to her."

"I AM your son, Mr. Perugino." Frank screamed out, annoyed over being ignored, "and you may not like it but I'm here to collect what's rightfully mine," he said with a self-satisfied smirk.

"Let me tell you what my mother told me in a letter she left behind after her recent death. YOU, Mr. Perugino, left my mom pregnant with no intention of helping her out." Frank furiously, with a hateful tone in his voice, stared down Leonardo, who sat up straight, resting his hands comfortably on his legs, but prepared to jump out of the chair at any given moment. Despite his age, Leonardo looked nothing like anyone who would easily give in to threats of the kind Frank was there to deliver.

"She was sent to the west coast by your people as if she was deported. Away from the people she knew, her family. Used and thrown away like a piece of trash," Frank continued.

With a calm voice Leonardo turned to Harry:

"Harry, we are done here. I'd like to have a word in privacy with this man Frank who claims he is my son."

Leonardo now stared down Frank. He was ready to take on the challenge of the man across the desk, who casually proclaimed he was the son Leonardo never knew he had. Leonardo was of course aware of the possibility. He had met a young woman right after arriving to New York but stayed away from her after being told she had ties to the west coast mafia families. Of course many other women had come and gone, wanting a piece of a successful and handsome Italian during his rise as a mobster. Yet he wasn't about to just accept that he had a son without having a man to man conversation about it, without anyone else in the room.

Harry, who knew both men's temper, wasn't comfortable leaving but had no say in the matter.

"I'll get in touch with you tomorrow, Leonardo," Harry reluctantly stood up from his chair next to the table, walked passed Frank, who with that unctuous look turned to Harry to say:

"Give my best to Joe, when and if you see him next. Oh, and please make sure you keep your woman at a safe distance from all the preying men out there."

Did he just threaten Maria? Harry felt the urge to hit the bastard. He reluctantly left the two men to settle their differences. The unease he felt was going to be confirmed once he sat in the car, starting to pull out of the farm to go to Maria's homecoming party.

He knew then something bad had happened. He knew he had to leave Italy with Maria as soon as possible. He also knew the final chapter of Leonardo's life story had been told and that it was time to go home.

The shots echoed out over the vineyard. Harry, who was just about to leave with Leonardo's driver who had been assigned to take him back and forth the last couple of days, saw a man run towards the house from a car that was parked nearby. Just as the man entered Leonardo's office another round of shots were fired. Three of Leonardo's men who had been working the field also ran to the house.

Harry's driver sped off, looked back at him through the rear view mirror and said:

"Let me get you to your hotel. Then get ready to leave Italy tomorrow. This isn't a safe place for you nor Signora Maria. I will contact you tomorrow morning to let you know what time you will be picked up. Please be ready early. We have a long ride back to Rome."

Harry said nothing. Just nodded that he had understood. The driver drove as fast as the narrow dirt road allowed to safely take Harry away from the violent and dangerous situation.

Harry was in a state of disbelief and shock. He had just witnessed how Frank had stormed into Leonardo's office claiming he was the son who had come back to grab what rightfully belonged to him. And now when asked to leave, Harry could only assume the meeting quickly had turned into a confrontation with a violent, deadly, outcome.

Of course it was possible that Leonardo could have fathered a son during his time in New York, and that he didn't know about it. It was clear that Frank wouldn't have put this much effort into locating Leonardo, even traveling to Perugia to face him, if he wasn't sure he was the forgotten son. Like Frank had said, his mother hadn't told him about Leonardo until after her death, leaving behind a letter and the photograph. The same photo Maria's mother once had received from Leonardo's mother, and the same one that now, after all these years, had ended up back in Perugia with Leonardo.

Leonardo who was believed to never have been married, nor have any children, seemed surprised, leading Harry to believe he wasn't aware of having fathered a son. Now facing Frank after all these years. If, Frank, was really his son he had followed in Leonardo's footsteps and became a mobster just like him.

Harry was worried about Leonardo. He never saw any guns in the office but realized a man like Leonardo, although living a retired and what seemed peaceful life, still was likely armed. Fearing the worse that this story was about to get a violent and tragic ending for the man he had gotten to know so well over the last week.

Harry didn't know what to do with the article that was about to be written as soon as he got back to the States.

How could he write an article about a man's life without knowing the ending?

Chapter Forty Nine

"What do you want, Frank, or whatever your name is?" "What makes you think I'll just fall for your story, calling me your father?" "What proof do you have?"

Frank didn't move. Just stood there for the longest time and stared at Leonardo, like a heavyweight championship match where neither boxer wants to make the first move. Then suddenly he broke the spell.

"I didn't come here for sympathy. I came here to take what rightfully belongs to me," he calmly but forcefully declared. "And for proof…what better proof than receiving a dying mother's confession and a picture of the family who had deserted her."

Frank was holding up the same picture Leonardo had received when Maria and Harry fist arrived, that Maria had found in the attic of her childhood home. The picture taken in 1944 with Leonardo as a young eighteen year-old with his family, mother, father, sister and little brother.

"And since I know Harry and Maria have the same picture and came all the way to Perugia to find you, I don't have to be a genius to figure out that you are the Leonardo I've been looking for. You destroyed my mother. I've been waiting to take what's mine and what you never cared about giving to my mother."

Leonardo moved his right arm and hand slowly up from his lap without Frank noticing the movement. He found the trigger on the Lupara short barrel shot gun that he used to kill his father and had his men attach under the table in case danger appeared. They made sure the gun was constantly cleaned and always loaded.

Frank froze for a moment. To stand in front of a man he never knew but clearly was the father he never met, was a lot to take in, even for Frank. Then, suddenly, like a deer staring into the head lights of an oncoming car approaching at high speed, he made a quick move with his right hand. He picked up and aimed the gun at Leonardo that he had concealed and secured by his belt in the back of his pants.

"Do you really think Mr. Perugino that I came to see my father who never wanted to see me. No, I came to kill you and take what's mine".

The first load of shots from the Lupara instantly killed Frank. Seconds later Frank's bodyguard came running in with his gun drawn and met the same fate as Frank when Leonardo blasted the second barrel of shots into him. Moments after, three men from the nearby field who had heard the shooting came running into the office finding Leonardo at his desk, not moving, just staring with blank eyes at the door.

The men quickly knew what to do for their Don Perugino. Roberto, the elderly of the three, went over to Leonardo while the others with speed and efficiency moved the bodies outside. No words were spoken. Everyone knew what needed to be done. No questions asked. The important thing was that Leonardo was safe.

"Don Perugino, we'll take care of this. I'll walk you over to your house so you may lay down for a while," said Roberto.

Roberto almost lifted Leonardo up from the chair and once he stood up on his now rather shaky legs, Roberto started walking him out of the office and the short walk to his living quarters. Once there, Leonardo's personal assistant and care taker waited for him, walked him to his bed and gave him the medicine he had been taking for the last six months.

The photograph stared down at him from its spot on the wall.

After all these years, the pent-up feeling of having to live his life with a secret he couldn't share was released. With a long strenuous exhale he could finally take that deep breath of fresh air again.

He looked at it with tired eyes - eyes that had seen so much pain, so much hope vanish too many times. The feeling of tasting the end, almost making it and being so close as if he could smell the victory even before crossing the finish line.

Too many years had passed, living his life chained to a lie; a lie necessitating fits of action and forced inaction. Many times he had felt shame, regret and suspicion of betrayal. It had troubled him to the point of wanting to end it all; but when it came to a moment of surety, there was too much at stake. Too many people depended on him sticking to the plan - the plan only he could see. As if everyone else's success fell on his willingness and strength to carry on.

What if? The question he never could answer. The road he had traveled on was unpaved and one that never could, for safety reasons, be paved. The only thing he could do was to travel along, keep going without looking back; without taking those exit ramps that had presented themselves to him over the years. It was painful every time he saw an exit sign, knowing very well he never could divert from the path. His tormented soul had finally reached the end of the road.

He reached up, grabbed the photograph, and took a last look at it before crumpling it in his right hand; the same hand that had squeezed the grip on a Lupara short barrel shotgun, twice.

Leonardo looked down at his fist, still firmly squeezed in a desperate attempt to free himself. Wanting to squeeze the life and lies of the photograph emitted. He was tired. He placed his head on the soft pillow, closed his eyes and realized after having kept it all inside, behind a wall of silence, that, finally, he had told his side of the story and freed himself from the heavy burden he had carried around all these years.

Chapter Fifty

A week had passed since Maria and Harry had arrived back in Cold Spring. Mrs. Rose, the nosy lady who thought of herself as the unofficial reporter for The Highlands Current, had told them about the burglary going wrong, as soon as she saw them arrive at Harry's apartment on 22 West Street.

She told them Joe had been killed in his own store early one Monday morning before even she was awake to "witness" the event. Shot to death and found the next day when Mrs. Rose had noticed that he hadn't opened up his store as usual. He was killed for the petty cash in his cash register, she explained with disappointment in her voice. She expected something more sinister since there had been a murder in town; something that hadn't happened in over fifty years. She had found out from the police that there were no traces of the perpetrator, who had at least twenty-four hours from the time the murder took place until it was discovered to disappear. Joe's store was closed on Mondays which was the reason for no one missing him until he was supposed to open up Tuesday morning. The police had little hope of finding the person who had broken in, surprised him and shot him dead. A burglary gone wrong.

For once Maria and Harry were happy to hear Mrs. Rose gossips and information about what had happened to Joe. Besides the fact that she found Maria's behavior, leaving for Italy so close to her husband's funeral, despicable, she was at the moment much more concerned about the violence in her small town. Not a day passed that first week without her pointing out that the village needed more police officers to patrol after dark. More volunteers walking the streets at night and for everyone to start locking their doors, something very few did in this peaceful town.

Maria was back at work at her Café and Harry was busy putting together his article for The New York Times. It was arranged to become a series of articles in the Sunday Times Magazine section. The problem he had was that he didn't know the end of the story. Harry didn't tell Maria about the shooting. He just told her that Leonardo sent his best wishes to Maria and that he was sorry he couldn't say goodbye to her in person.

Ten days after arriving back to Cold Spring, Harry was ready to submit his story when a letter was delivered by Tom, the mail man, Mrs. Rose's best friend and "informant." Harry immediately noticed it was postmarked Perugia, Italy with no return address. He quickly opened it and when unfolding the letter, a crumpled photograph fell to the floor. The photograph was of the Perugino family, the one picture Maria had given him on their first day of meeting Leonardo.

Harry started reading the letter.

Chapter Fifty One

Dear Harry,

When you read this you will know I'm still alive. I understand you must have a few more unanswered questions about what happened that last day when my son Frank, who I knew nothing about, showed up.

But before I go any further I need to tell you I have only a few more days to live.

I was diagnosed with an aggressive cancer six months ago. There's nothing more to live for. I did what I had to do with the options I had and I'm relieved my life is ending having had the opportunity to tell my story.

Killing my father was something that liberated my family, whom I so dearly miss and love. Killing the idiot who raped my sister, brought me nothing but redemption. But the price I paid was high. Very high. Never being able to see my family, and now not able to say farewell, is a sacrifice I hope no one else will ever have to make. Killing my own son is a tragedy I won't be able to live with and I'm happy God has made plans for me to leave this world quite soon.

By the time you publish my story, and my family reads and understand why I had to live in hiding the rest of my life after leaving them back in 1953, I ask you to leave out the end. This is my last dying wish that only you, me and God will ever know. Killing my father was the ticket for my family's freedom. Killing my son in self-defense, even after knowing what he had become, was something I'd rather not talk about, or for it to be part of my legacy. It will be read by not only my family but by a world back in the US I no longer know. Please honor my wish to let that episode of my life die with me.

Send my love to Maria. Take good care of her. She is like her mother, an Angel, who spreads joy and warmth around her. You both made my last couple of weeks memorable and happy. Happy to have been able to tell my story. And whatever my family may think about me and my actions I won't die without them knowing what happened to me and the decisions I made for my "famiglia."

Sincerely,

Leonardo Perugino

Harry read the letter several times. He made the decision to honor Leonardo's wish, saving the letter and photograph but keeping it a secret from everyone, including Maria, as promised.

Before the article was published, Maria received a call from her relatives in Perugia. Her Aunt told her Leonardo Perugino had passed, peacefully, only days after Maria and Harry had left and after he apparently had received news about an inoperable cancer six months before.

Epilogue – Cold Spring in the fall of 2015

Harry wrote a well received New York Times article. His name was not only recognized in the small town of Cold Spring, but in various places in the States and beyond. Even though he was sought after to write articles in all the big newspapers and magazines, he had decided to take on a new challenge.

Spending time with Leonardo made him want to find out more about the Swedish roots his mother had told him about. His Swedish father had left when Harry was only two, leaving his mother to do the work of both parents. Something she had done with pride and courage. Harry had never met his father since that day.

Harry had made plans to bring Maria along on a trip back to Sweden around Christmas time, in an attempt to locate his father, if he was still alive.

Little did he know this journey was going to reveal huge secrets hidden away by time.

It could be his most personal and dangerous endeavor he had ever begun.

But for now, Harry was very happy being back home in Cold Spring with the love of his life.

Sweet Maria's Café was the place to be for morning coffee… and romance.

THE END.

Acknowledgement

Writing this book was the most challenging and rewarding experience of my life.

I learned much I didn't know about myself; emotions, love, and hate – feelings we too often hide, forget to share, and even worse, deny.

I'm grateful to the many people and places that opened up allowing me to hear their voices, stories, and history.

I owe an incredible amount to my editors Jay and Linda Spear who read more drafts than I thought was possible, offered important feedback, from questioning the choice of a word to doubting the wisdom of deleting entire paragraphs, or even chapters.

Their encouragement and help was of crucial importance for me in order to finish *"A Mindful Death"*.

www.aHarryAndersonMystery.com